The Voyages of Sindbad

TRANSLATED BY N. J. DAWOOD

PENGUIN EPICS

PENGUIN BOOKS

Published by the Penguin Group
Penguin Books Ltd, 80 Strand, London WC2R ORL, England
Penguin Group (USA) Inc., 375 Hudson Street, New York, New York 10014, USA
Penguin Group (Canada), 90 Eglinton Avenue East, Suite 700, Toronto, Ontario, Canada M4P 2Y3
(a division of Pearson Penguin Canada Inc.)
Penguin Ireland, 25 St Stephen's Green, Dublin 2, Ireland (a division of Penguin Books Ltd)
Penguin Group (Australia), 250 Camberwell Road, Camberwell, Victoria 3124, Australia
(a division of Pearson Australia Group Pty Ltd)
Penguin Books India Pvt Ltd, 11 Community Centre, Panchsheel Park, New Delhi – 110 017, India
Penguin Group (NZ), cnr Airborne and Rosedale Roads, Albany,
Auckland 1310, New Zealand (a division of Pearson New Zealand Ltd)
Penguin Books (South Africa) (Pty) Ltd, 24 Sturdee Avenue,
Rosebank, Johannesburg 2196, South Africa

Penguin Books Ltd, Registered Offices: 80 Strand, London WC2R ORL, England

www.penguin.com

This translation of *The Thousand and One Nights* first published in Penguin Classics 1954
Revised edition published 1973
This extract published in Penguin Books 2006

I

Translation copyright © N. J. Dawood, 1954, 1973
All rights reserved

Taken from the Penguin Classics edition of *The Thousand and One Nights*,
translated and edited by N. J. Dawood

Typeset by Rowland Phototypesetting Ltd, Bury St Edmunds, Suffolk
Printed in England by Clays Ltd, St Ives plc

ISBN-13: 978-0-141-02644-2
ISBN-10: 0-141-02644-8

Contents

Note

Taken from *The Thousand and One Nights* – the stories told by Shahrazad over a thousand and one nights to delay her execution by King Shahriyar – *The Voyages of Sindbad* appeared in their final form in the seventeenth century in Arabic.

The Voyages of Sindbad the Sailor

Once upon a time, in the reign of the Caliph Haroun al-Rashid, there lived in the city of Baghdad a poor man who earned his living by carrying burdens upon his head. He was called Sindbad the Porter.

One day, as he was staggering under a heavy load in the sweltering heat of the summer sun, he passed by a merchant's house that stood in a pleasant, shaded spot on the roadside. The ground before it was well swept and watered; and Sindbad, seeing a broad wooden bench just outside the gates, put down his load and sat there to rest awhile and to wipe away the sweat which trickled down his forehead. A cool and fragrant breeze blew through the doorway, and from within came the melodious strains of the lute and voices singing. They mingled with the choirs of birds warbling hymns to Allah in various tongues and tunes: curlews and pigeons, merles and bulbuls and turtle-doves.

Moved with great joy, he went up to the door and, looking within, saw in the centre of the noble courtyard a beautiful garden, around which stood numerous slaves and eunuchs and such an array of attendants as can be found only in the courts of illustrious kings. And all about the place floated the aroma of the choicest meats and wines.

Still marvelling at the splendour of what he saw,

Sindbad lifted up his burden and was about to go his way when there came from within a handsome and well-dressed little page, who took him by the hand, saying: 'Pray come in; my master wishes to speak with you.'

The porter politely declined; but the lad would take no refusal. So Sindbad left his burden in the vestibule with the door-keeper and followed the page into the house.

He was conducted into a magnificent and spacious hall, where an impressive company of nobles and mighty sheikhs were seated according to rank at tables spread with the daintiest meats and richest wines, and gaily decked with flowers and fruit. On one side of the hall sat beautiful slave-girls who sang and made music; and to the fore reclined the host, a venerable old man whose beard was touched with silver. Bewildered at the grandeur and majesty of all that he beheld, the porter thought to himself: 'By Allah, this must either be a corner of Paradise or the palace of some mighty king!'

Sindbad courteously greeted the distinguished assembly and, kissing the ground before them, wished them joy and prosperity. He then stood in silence with eyes cast down.

The master of the house welcomed him kindly and bade him draw near and be seated. He ordered his slaves to set before the porter a choice of delicate foods and pressed him to eat. After pronouncing the blessing Sindbad fell to, and when he had eaten his fill washed his hands and thanked the old sheikh for his hospitality.

'You are welcome to this house, my friend,' said the host, 'and may this day bring you joy. We would gladly know your name and calling.'

'My name is Sindbad,' he answered, 'by trade a porter.'

'How strange a chance!' smiled the old man. 'For my name, too, is Sindbad. They call me Sindbad the Sailor, and marvel at my strange history. Presently, my brother, you shall hear the tale of my fortunes and all the hardships that I suffered before I rose to my present state and became the lord of this mansion where we are now assembled. For only after long toil, fearful ordeals, and dire peril did I achieve this fame. Seven voyages I made in all, each a story of such marvel as confounds the reason and fills the soul with wonder. All that befell me had been pre-ordained; and that which the moving hand of Fate has written no mortal power can revoke.'

The First Voyage of Sindbad the Sailor

Know, my friends, that my father was the chief merchant of this city and one of its richest men. He died whilst I was still a child, leaving me great wealth and many estates and farmlands. As soon as I came of age and had control of my inheritance, I took to extravagant living. I clad myself in the costliest robes, ate and drank sumptuously, and consorted with reckless prodigals of my own age, thinking that this mode of life would endure for ever.

It was not long before I awoke from my heedless folly to find that I had frittered away my entire fortune. I was stricken with horror and dismay at the gravity of my plight, and bethought myself of a proverb of our master Solomon son of David (may peace be upon them both!)

which my father often used to cite: 'The day of death is better than the day of birth, a live dog is better than a dead lion, and the grave is better than poverty.' I sold the remainder of my lands and my household chattels for the sum of three thousand dirhams, and, fortifying myself with hope and courage, resolved to travel abroad and trade in foreign lands.

I bought a large quantity of merchandise and made preparations for a long voyage. Then I set sail together with a company of merchants in a river-ship bound for Basrah. There we put to sea and, voyaging many days and nights from isle to isle and from shore to shore, buying and selling and bartering wherever the ship anchored, we came at length to a little island as fair as the Garden of Eden. Here the captain of our ship cast anchor and put out the landing-planks.

The passengers went ashore and set to work to light a fire. Some busied themselves with cooking and washing, some fell to eating and drinking and making merry, while others, like myself, set out to explore the island. Whilst we were thus engaged we suddenly heard the captain cry out to us from the ship: 'All aboard, quickly! Abandon everything and run for your lives! The mercy of Allah be upon you, for this is no island but a gigantic whale floating on the bosom of the sea, on whose back the sands have settled and trees have grown since the world was young! When you lit the fire it felt the heat and stirred. Make haste, I say; or soon the whale will plunge into the sea and you will all be lost!'

Hearing the captain's cries, the passengers made for the ship in panic-stricken flight, leaving behind their cooking-pots and other belongings. Some reached the ship in safety, but others did not; for suddenly the island shook beneath our feet and, submerged by mountainous waves, sank with all that stood upon it to the bottom of the roaring ocean.

Together with my unfortunate companions I was engulfed by the merciless tide; but Providence came to my aid, casting in my way a great wooden trough which had been used by the ship's company for washing. Impelled by that instinct which makes all mortals cling to life, I held fast to the trough and, bestriding it firmly, paddled away with my feet as the waves tossed and buffeted me on every side. Meanwhile the captain hoisted sail and set off with the other passengers. I followed the ship with my eyes until it vanished from sight, and I resigned myself to certain death.

Darkness soon closed in upon the ocean. All that night and throughout the following day I drifted on, lashed by the wind and the waves, until the trough brought me to the steep shores of a densely wooded island, where trees hung over the sea.

I caught hold of one of the branches and with its aid managed to clamber ashore after fighting so long for my life. Finding myself again on dry land, I realized that I had lost the use of my legs, and my feet began to smart with the bites of fish.

Worn out by anguish and exertion, I sank into a death-like slumber; and it was not until the following morning when the sun rose that I came to my senses. But my feet were so sore and swollen that I could move about only by crawling on my knees. By good fortune, however, the island had an abundance of fruit-trees, which provided me with sustenance, and many springs of fresh water, so that after a few days my body was restored to strength and my spirit revived. I cut myself a staff from the branch of a tree, and with its aid set out to explore the island and to admire the many goodly things which Allah had planted on its soil.

One day, as I was roaming about the beach in an unfamiliar part of the island, I caught sight of a strange object in the distance which appeared to be some wild beast or sea-monster. As I drew nearer and looked more closely at it, I saw that it was a noble mare of an uncommonly high stature haltered to a tree. On seeing me the mare gave an ear-splitting neigh which made me take to my heels in terror. Presently a man emerged from the ground and pursued me, shouting: 'Who are you and whence have you come? What are you doing here?'

'Sir,' I replied, 'I am a luckless voyager, abandoned in the middle of the sea; but it was Allah's will that I should be rescued from the fury of the waves and cast upon this island.'

The stranger took me by the hand and bade me follow him. He led me to a subterranean cavern and, after asking me to be seated, he placed some food before me and invited me to eat. When I had eaten my fill he questioned me about the fortunes of my voyage, and I related to him all that had befallen me from first to last.

'But, pray tell me, sir,' I inquired, as my host marvelled at my adventure, 'what is the reason of your vigil here and for what purpose is this mare tethered on the beach?'

'Know,' he replied, 'that I am one of the many grooms

of King Mahrajan. We have charge of all his horses and are stationed in different parts of this island. Each month, on the night of the full moon, we tether all the virgin mares on the beach and hide in shelters near by. Presently the sea-horses scent the mares and, after emerging from the water, leap upon the beasts and cover them. Then they try to drag them away into the sea. But this they fail to do, as the mares are securely roped. With angry cries the sea-horses attack the mares and kick them with their hind legs. At this point we rush from our hiding-places and drive the sea-horses back into the water. The mares then conceive and bear colts and fillies of inestimable worth. Tonight,' he added, 'when we have completed our task, I shall take you to our King and show you our city. Allah be praised for this happy encounter; for had you not chanced to meet us you would have surely come to grief in the solitude of these wild regions.'

I thanked him with all my heart and called down blessings upon him. Whilst we were thus engaged in conversation we heard a dreadful cry in the distance. The groom quickly snatched up his sword and buckler and rushed out, shouting aloud and banging his sword on his shield. Thereupon several other grooms came out from their hiding-places, brandishing their spears and yelling at the top of their voices. The sea-horse, who had just covered the mare, took fright at this tumult and plunged, like a buffalo, headlong into the sea, where he disappeared beneath the water.

As we sat on the ground to recover our breath, the other grooms, each leading a mare, approached us. My companion explained to them the circumstances of my presence, and, after exchanging greetings, we rode to the city of King Mahrajan.

As soon as the King was informed of my arrival he summoned me to his presence. He marvelled at my story, saying: 'By Allah, my son, your preservation has been truly miraculous. Praise be to the Highest for your deliverance!'

Thenceforth I rose rapidly in the King's favour and soon became a trusted courtier. He vested me with robes of honour and appointed me Comptroller of Shipping at the port of his kingdom. And during my sojourn in that realm I earned the gratitude of the poor and the humble for my readiness to intercede for them with the King.

There I witnessed many prodigies and met travellers from different foreign lands. One day I entered the King's chamber and found him entertaining a company of Indians. I exchanged greetings with them and questioned them about their country. In the course of conversation I was astonished to learn that there were no fewer than seventy-two different castes in India. The noblest of these castes is known as Shakiriyah, and its members are renowned for piety and fair dealing. Another caste are the Brahmins. They are skilled breeders of camels, horses, and cattle, and, though they abstain from wine, they are a merry and pleasure-loving people.

Not far from the King's dominions there is a little island where at night is heard a mysterious beating of drums and clash of tambourines. Travellers and men from neighbouring isles told me that its inhabitants were a shrewd and diligent race.

In those distant seas I once saw a fish two hundred cubits in length, and another with a head that resembled an owl's. This I saw with my own eyes, and many other things no less strange and wondrous.

Whenever I walked along the quay I talked with the sailors and travellers from far countries, inquiring whether any of them had heard tell of the city of Baghdad and how far off it lay; for I never lost hope that I should one day find my way back to my native land. But there was none who knew of that city; and as the days dragged by, my longing for home weighed heavy upon my heart.

One day, however, as I stood on the wharf, leaning upon my staff and gazing out to sea, a ship bearing a large company of merchants came sailing into the harbour. As soon as it was moored, the sails were furled and landing-planks put out. The crew began to unload the cargo, and I stood by entering up the merchandise in my register. When they had done, I asked the captain if all the goods had now been brought ashore.

'Sir,' he replied, 'in the ship's hold I still have a few bales which belonged to a merchant who was drowned at an early stage of our voyage. We shall put them up for sale and take the money to his kinsmen in Baghdad, the City of Peace.'

'What was the merchant's name?' I demanded.

'Sindbad,' he answered.

I looked more closely into his face, and, recognizing him at once, uttered a joyful cry.

'Why!' I exclaimed, 'I am Sindbad, the self-same owner of these goods, who was left to drown with many others when the great whale plunged into the sea. But through the grace of Allah I was cast by the waves onto the shores of this island, where I found favour with the King and became Comptroller at this port. I am the true owner of these goods, which are my only possessions in this world.'

'By Allah,' cried the captain, 'is there no longer any faith or honesty in man? I have but to mention a dead man's goods and you claim them for your own! Why, we saw Sindbad drown before our very eyes. Dare you lay claim to his property?'

'I pray you, captain,' I rejoined, 'listen to my story and you shall soon learn the whole truth.' I then recounted to him all the details of the voyage from the day we set sail from Basrah till we cast anchor off the treacherous island and reminded him of a certain matter that had passed between us.

The captain and the passengers now recognized me, and all congratulated me on my escape, saying: 'Allah has granted you a fresh span of life!'

At once my goods were brought ashore and I rejoiced to find the bales intact and sealed as I had left them. I selected some of the choicest and most precious articles as presents for King Mahrajan, and had them carried by the sailors to the royal palace, where I laid them at his feet. I informed the King of the unexpected arrival of my ship and the happy recovery of all my goods. He marvelled greatly at this chance, and, in return for my presents, bestowed upon me priceless treasures.

I sold my wares at a substantial profit and re-equipped myself with the finest produce of that island. When all was ready for the homeward voyage I presented myself at the King's court, and, thanking him for the many favours he had shown me, begged leave to return to my land and people.

Then we set sail, trusting in Allah and propitious Fortune; and after voyaging many days and nights we at length arrived safely in Basrah.

I spent but a few days in that town and then, loaded with treasure, set out for Baghdad, the City of Peace. I was overjoyed to be back in my native city, and hastening to my old street entered my own house, where by and by all my friends and kinsmen came to greet me.

I bought fine houses and rich farm-lands, concubines and eunuchs and black slaves, and became richer than I had ever been before. I kept open house for my old companions, and, soon forgetting the hardships of my voyage, resumed with new zest my former mode of living.

That is the story of the first of my adventures. Tomorrow, if Allah wills, I shall relate to you the tale of my second voyage.

The day was drawing to its close, and Sindbad the Sailor invited Sindbad the Porter to join the guests in the evening meal. When the feast was finished he gave him a hundred pieces of gold, saying: 'You have delighted us with your company this day.'

The porter thanked him for his generous gift and departed, pondering over the vicissitudes of fortune and marvelling at all that he had heard.

Next morning he went again to the house of his benefactor, who received him courteously and seated him by his side. Presently the other guests arrived, and when they had feasted and made merry, Sindbad the Sailor began:

The Second Voyage of Sindbad the Sailor

For some time after my return to Baghdad I continued to lead a joyful and carefree life, but it was not long before I felt an irresistible longing to travel again about the world and to visit distant cities and islands in quest of profit and adventure. So I bought a great store of merchandise and, after making preparations for departure, sailed down the Tigris to Basrah. There I embarked, together with a band of merchants, in a fine new vessel, well-equipped and manned by a sturdy crew, which set sail the same day.

Aided by a favourable wind, we voyaged for many days and nights from port to port and from island to island, selling and bartering our goods, and haggling with merchants and officials wherever we cast anchor. At length Destiny carried our ship to the shores of an uninhabited island, rich in fruit and flowers, and jubilant with the singing of birds and the murmur of crystal streams.

Here passengers and crew went ashore, and we all set off to enjoy the delights of the island. I strolled through the green meadows, leaving my companions far behind, and sat down in a shady thicket to eat a simple meal by a spring of water. Lulled by the soft and fragrant breeze which blew around me, I lay upon the grass and presently fell asleep.

I cannot tell how long I slept, but when I awoke I saw none of my fellow-travellers, and soon realized that the ship had sailed away without anyone noticing my absence. I ran in frantic haste towards the sea, and on reaching the shore saw the vessel, a white speck upon the vast blue ocean, dissolving into the far horizon.

Broken with terror and despair, I threw myself upon the sand, wailing: 'Now your end has come, Sindbad! The jar that drops a second time is sure to break!' I cursed the day I bade farewell to the joys of a contented life and bitterly repented my folly in venturing again upon the hazards and hardships of the sea, after having so narrowly escaped death in my first voyage.

At length, resigning myself to my doom, I rose and, after wandering about aimlessly for some time, climbed into a tall tree. From its top I gazed long in all directions, but could see nothing save the sky, the trees, the birds, the sands, and the boundless ocean. As I scanned the interior of the island more closely, however, I gradually became aware of some white object looming in the distance. At once I climbed down the tree and made my way towards it. Drawing nearer, I found to my astonishment that it was a white dome of extraordinary dimensions. I walked all round it, but could find no door or entrance of any kind; and so smooth and slippery was its surface that any attempt to climb it would have been fruitless. I walked round it again, and, making a mark in the sand near its base, found that its circumference measured more than fifty paces.

Whilst I was thus engaged the sun was suddenly hidden from my view as by a great cloud and the world grew dark around me. I lifted up my eyes towards the sky, and was confounded to see a gigantic bird with enormous wings which, as it flew through the air, screened the sun and hid it from the island.

The sight of this prodigy instantly called to my mind a story I had heard in my youth from pilgrims and adventurers – how in a far island dwelt a bird of monstrous size called the roc, which fed its young on elephants; and at once I realized that the white dome was none other than a roc's egg. In a twinkling the bird alighted upon the egg, covering it completely with its wings and stretching out its legs behind it on the ground. And in this posture it went to sleep. (Glory to Him who never sleeps!)

Rising swiftly, I unwound my turban from my head, then doubled it and twisted it into a rope with which I securely bound myself by the waist to one of the great talons of the monster. 'Perchance this bird,' I thought, 'will carry me away to a civilized land; wherever I am set down, it will surely be better than a solitary island.'

I lay awake all night, fearing to close my eyes lest the bird should fly away with me while I slept. At daybreak the roc rose from the egg, and, spreading its wings, took to the air with a terrible cry. I clung fast to its talon as it winged its way through the void and soared higher and higher until it almost touched the heavens. After some time it began to drop, and sailing swiftly downwards came to earth on the brow of steep hill.

Trembling with fear, I hastened to untie my turban before the roc became aware of my presence. Scarcely had I released myself when the monster darted off towards a great black object lying near and, clutching it in its fearful claws, took wing again. As it rose in the air I was astonished to see that this was a serpent of immeasurable length; and with its prey the bird vanished from sight.

Looking around, I found myself on a precipitous hill-side overlooking an exceedingly deep and vast valley. On all sides towered craggy mountains whose beetling summits no man could ever scale. I was stricken with fear and repented my rashness. 'Would that I had remained in that island!' I thought to myself. 'There at least I lacked neither fruit nor water, while these barren steeps offer nothing to eat or drink. No sooner do I escape from one peril than I find myself in another more grievous. There is no strength or help save in Allah!'

When I had made my way down the hill I marvelled to see the ground thickly covered with the rarest diamonds, so that the entire valley blazed with a glorious light. Here and there among the glittering stones, however, coiled deadly snakes and vipers, dread keepers of the fabulous treasure. Thicker and longer than giant palm-trees, they could have swallowed whole elephants at one gulp. They were crawling back into their sunless dens, for by day they hid themselves from their enemies the rocs and the eagles and moved about only at night.

Overwhelmed with horror, and oblivious of hunger and fatigue, I roamed the valley all day searching with infinite caution for a shelter where I might pass the night. At dusk I came upon a narrow-mouthed cave, into which I crawled, blocking its entrance from within by a great stone. I thought to myself: 'Here I shall be safe tonight. When tomorrow comes, let Destiny do its worst.'

Scarcely had I advanced a few steps, when I saw at

the far end of the cave an enormous serpent coiled in a great knot round its eggs. My hair stood on end and I was transfixed with terror. Seeing no way of escape, however, I put my trust in Allah and kept vigil all night. At daybreak I rolled back the stone and staggered out of the cave, reeling like a drunken man.

As I thus stumbled along I noticed a great joint of flesh come tumbling down into the valley from rock to rock. Upon closer inspection I found this to be a whole sheep, skinned and drawn. I was deeply perplexed at the mystery, for there was not a soul in sight; but at that very moment there flashed across my mind the memory of a story I had once heard from travellers who had visited the Diamond Mountains – how men obtained the diamonds from this treacherous and inaccessible valley by a strange device. Before sunrise they would throw whole carcasses of sheep from the top of the mountains, so that the gems on which they fell penetrated the soft flesh and became embedded in it. At midday rocs and mighty vultures would swoop down upon the mutton and carry it away in their talons to their nests in the mountain heights. With a great clamour the merchants would then rush at the birds and force them to drop the meat and fly away, after which it would only remain to look through the carcasses and pick out the diamonds.

As I recalled this story a plan of escape formed in my mind. I selected a great quantity of priceless stones and hid them all about me, filling my pockets with them and pressing them into the folds of my belt and garments. Then I unrolled my turban, stuffed it with more diamonds, twisted it into a rope as I had done before, and, lying down below the carcass, bound it firmly to my chest. I had not remained long in that position when I suddenly felt myself lifted from the ground by the talons of a huge vulture which had tightly closed upon the meat. The bird climbed higher and higher and finally alighted upon the top of a mountain. As soon as it began to tear at the flesh there arose from behind the neighbouring rocks a great tumult, at which the bird took fright and flew away. At once I freed myself and sprang to my feet, with face and clothes all bloody.

I saw a man come running to the spot and stop in alarm as he saw me. Without uttering a word he cautiously bent over the carcass to examine it, eyeing me suspiciously all the while; but finding no diamonds, he wrung his hands and lifted up his arms, crying: 'O heavy loss! Allah, in whom alone dwell all power and majesty, defend us from the wiles of the Evil One!'

Before I could explain my presence the man, shaking with fear, turned to me and asked: 'Who are you, and how came you here?'

'Do not be alarmed, sir,' I replied, 'I am no evil spirit, but an honest man, a merchant by profession. My story is an extraordinary one, and the adventure which has brought me to these mountains surpasses in wonder all the marvels that men have seen or heard of. But first pray accept some of these diamonds, which I myself gathered in the fearful valley below.'

I took some splendid jewels from my pocket and offered them to him, saying: 'These will bring you all the riches you can desire.'

The owner of the bait was overjoyed at the unexpected

gift; he warmly thanked me and called down blessings upon me. Whilst we were thus talking, several other merchants came up from the mountain-side. They crowded round us, listening in amazement to my story, and congratulated me, saying: 'By Allah, your escape was a miracle; for no man has ever set foot in that valley and returned alive. Allah alone be praised for your salvation.'

The merchants then led me to their tent. They gave me food and drink and there I slept soundly for many hours. Early next day we set out from our tent and, after journeying over a vast range of mountains, came at length to the seashore. After a short voyage we arrived in a pleasant, densely wooded island, covered with trees so huge that beneath one of them a hundred men could shelter from the sun. It is from these trees that the aromatic substance known as camphor is extracted. The trunks are hollowed out, and the sap oozes drop by drop into vessels which are placed beneath, soon curdling into a crystal gum.

In that island I saw a gigantic beast called the karkadan, or rhinoceros, which grazes in the fields like a cow or buffalo. Taller than a camel, it has a single horn in the middle of its forehead, and upon this horn Nature has carved the likeness of a man. The karkadan attacks the elephant and, impaling it upon its horn, carries it aloft from place to place until its victim dies. Before long, however, the elephant's fat melts in the heat of the sun and, dripping down into the karkadan's eyes, puts out its sight, so that the beast blunders helplessly along and finally drops dead. Then the roc swoops down upon both animals and carries them off to its nest in the high mountains. I also saw many strange breeds of buffalo in that island.

I sold a part of my diamonds for a large sum and exchanged more for a vast quantity of merchandise. Then we set sail and, trading from port to port and from island to island, at length arrived safely in Basrah. After a few days' sojourn there I set out upstream to Baghdad, the City of Peace.

Loaded with precious goods and the finest of my diamonds, I hastened to my old street and, entering my own house, rejoiced to see my friends and kinsfolk. I gave them gold and presents, and distributed alms among the poor of the city.

I soon forgot the perils and hardships of my travels and took again to sumptuous living. I ate well, dressed well, and kept open house for innumerable gallants and boon companions.

From far and near men came to hear me speak of my adventures and to learn the news of foreign lands from me. All were astounded at the dangers I had escaped and wished me joy of my return. Such was my second voyage.

Tomorrow, my friends, if Allah wills, I shall relate to you the extraordinary tale of my third voyage.

The famous mariner ended. The guests marvelled at his story.

When the evening feast was over, Sindbad the Sailor gave Sindbad the Porter a hundred pieces of gold, which he took with thanks and many blessings, and departed, lost in wonderment at all he had heard.

Next day the porter rose and, after reciting his morning

prayers, went to the house of his illustrious friend, who received him kindly and seated him by his side. And when all the guests had assembled, Sindbad the Sailor began:

The Third Voyage of Sindbad the Sailor

Know, my friends, that for some time after my return I continued to lead a happy and tranquil life, but I soon grew weary of my idle existence in Baghdad and once again longed to roam the world in quest of profit and adventure. Unmindful of the dangers of ambition and worldly greed, I resolved to set out on another voyage. I provided myself with a great store of goods and, after taking them down the Tigris, set sail from Basrah, together with a band of honest merchants.

The voyage began prosperously. We called at many foreign ports, trading profitably with our merchandise. One day, however, whilst we were sailing in mid ocean, we heard the captain of our ship, who was on deck scanning the horizon, suddenly burst out in a loud lament. He beat himself about the face, tore his beard, and rent his clothes.

'We are lost!' he cried, as we crowded round him. 'The treacherous wind has driven us off our course towards that island which you see before you. It is the Isle of the Zughb, where dwell a race of dwarfs more akin to apes than men, from whom no voyager has ever escaped alive!'

Scarcely had he uttered these words when a multitude of ape-like savages appeared on the beach and began to swim out towards the ship. In a few moments they were upon us, thick as a swarm of locusts. Barely four spans in height, they were the ugliest of living creatures, with little gleaming yellow eyes and bodies thickly covered with black fur. And so numerous were they that we did not dare to provoke them or attempt to drive them away, lest they should set upon us and kill us to a man by force of numbers.

They scrambled up the masts, gnawing the cables with their teeth and biting them to shreds. Then they seized the helm and steered the vessel to their island. When the ship had run ashore, the dwarfs carried us one by one to the beach, and, promptly pushing off again, climbed on board and sailed away.

Disconsolately we set out to search for food and water, and by good fortune came upon some fruit-trees and a running stream. Here we refreshed ourselves, and then wandered about the island until at length we saw far off among the trees a massive building, where we hoped to pass the night in safety. Drawing nearer, we found that it was a towering palace surrounded by a lofty wall, with a great ebony door which stood wide open. We entered the spacious courtyard, and to our surprise found it deserted. In one corner lay a great heap of bones, and on the far side we saw a broad bench, an open oven, pots and pans of enormous size, and many iron spits for roasting.

Exhausted and sick at heart, we lay down in the courtyard and were soon overcome by sleep. At sunset we were awakened by a noise like thunder. The earth shook beneath our feet and we saw a colossal black giant approaching from the doorway. He was a fearsome sight

– tall as a palm-tree, with red eyes burning in his head like coals of fire; his mouth was a dark well, with lips that drooped like a camel's loosely over his chest, whilst his ears, like a pair of large round discs, hung back over his shoulders: his fangs were as long as the tusks of a boar and his nails were like the claws of a lion.

The sight of this monster struck terror to our hearts. We cowered motionless on the ground as we watched him stride across the yard and sit down on the bench. For a few moments he eyed us one by one in silence; then he rose and, reaching out towards me, lifted me up by the neck and began feeling my body as a butcher would a lamb. Finding me little more than skin and bone, however, he flung me to the ground and, picking up each of my companions in turn, pinched and prodded them and set them down until at last he came to the captain.

Now the captain was a corpulent fellow, tall and broad-shouldered. The giant seemed to like him well. He gripped him as a butcher grips a fatted ram and broke his neck under his foot. Then he thrust an iron spit through his body from mouth to backside and, lighting a great fire in the oven, carefully turned his victim round and round before it. When the flesh was finely roasted, the ogre tore the body to pieces with his fingernails as though it were a pullet, and devoured it limb by limb, gnawing the bones and flinging them against the wall. The monster then stretched himself out on the bench and soon fell fast asleep. His snores were as loud as the grunts and gurgles that issue from the throat of a slaughtered beast.

Thus he slept all night, and when morning came he

rose and went out of the palace, leaving us half-crazed with terror.

As soon as we were certain that the monster had gone, we began lamenting our evil fortune. 'Would that we had been drowned in the sea or killed by the apes!' we cried. 'That would surely have been better than the foul death which now awaits us! But that which Allah has ordained must surely come to pass.'

We left the palace to search for some hiding-place, but could find no shelter in any part of the island, and had no choice but to return to the palace in the evening. Night came, and with it the black giant, announcing his approach by a noise like thunder. No sooner had he entered than he snatched up one of the merchants and prepared his supper in the same way as the night before. Then, stretching himself out to sleep, he snored the night away.

Next morning, when the giant had gone, we discussed our desperate plight.

'By Allah,' cried one of the merchants, 'let us rather throw ourselves into the sea than remain alive to be roasted and eaten!'

'Listen, my friends,' said another. 'We must kill this monster. For only by destroying him can we end his wickedness and save good Moslems from his barbarous cruelty.'

This proposal was received with general approbation; so I rose in my turn and addressed the company. 'If we are all agreed to kill this monster,' I said, 'let us first build a raft on which we can escape from this island as soon as we have sent his soul to damnation. Perchance our raft will take us to some other island, where we can board a ship bound for our country. If we are drowned, we shall at least escape roasting and die a martyr's death.'

'By Allah,' cried the others, 'that is a wise plan.'

Setting to work at once, we hauled several logs from the great pile of wood stacked beside the oven and carried them out of the palace. Then we fastened them together into a raft, which we left ready on the seashore.

In the evening the earth shook beneath our feet as the black giant burst in upon us, barking and snarling like a mad dog. Once more he seized upon the stoutest of my companions and prepared his meal. When he had eaten his fill, he stretched himself upon the bench as was his custom and soon fell fast asleep.

Noiselessly we now rose, took two of the great iron spits from the oven, and thrust them into the fire. As soon as they were red hot we carried them over to the snoring monster and plunged their sharpened ends deep into his eyes, exerting our united weight from above to push them home. The giant gave a deafening shriek which filled our hearts with terror and cast us back on the ground many yards away. Totally blinded, he leapt up from the bench groping for us with outstretched hands, while we nimbly dodged his frantic clutches. In despair he felt his way to the ebony door and staggered out of the yard, groaning in agonies of pain.

Without losing a moment we made off towards the beach. As soon as we reached the water we launched our raft and jumped aboard; but scarcely had we rowed a few yards when we saw the blind savage running towards us, guided by a foul hag of his own kind. On reaching the shore they stood howling threats and curses at us for a while, and then caught up massive boulders and hurled them at our raft with stupendous force. Missile followed missile until all my companions, save two, were drowned; but we three who escaped soon contrived to paddle beyond the range of their fury.

Lashed by the waves, we drifted on in the open sea for a whole day and a whole night until we were cast upon the shore of another island. Half-dead with hunger and exhaustion, we threw ourselves upon the sand and fell asleep.

Next morning, when we awoke, we found ourselves encircled by a serpent of prodigious size, which lay about us in a knotted coil. Before we could move a limb the beast suddenly reared its head and, opening wide its deadly jaws, seized one of my companions and swallowed him to the shoulders, then it gulped him down entirely, and we heard his ribs crack in its belly. Presently, however, the serpent unwound its loathsome body and, heedless of my companion and myself, glided away, leaving us stricken with grief at the horrible fate of our comrade and amazed at our own narrow escape.

'By Allah,' we cried, 'we have fled from one form of death only to meet with another as hideous. How shall we now escape this serpent? There is no strength or help save in Allah!'

The warmth of the new-born day inspired us with fresh courage, and we struck inland to search for food and water. Before nightfall we climbed into a tall tree, and perched ourselves as best we could upon the topmost branches. But as soon as darkness fell we heard a fearful hissing and a noise of heavy movement on the ground; and in a twinkling the serpent had seized my friend and gulped him down, cracking all his bones in its belly. Then the vile creature slid down the tree and disappeared among the vegetation. That was the end of the last of my companions.

At daybreak I climbed down from my hiding-place. My first thought was to throw myself into the sea and thus end a life which had already endured more than its share of hardships and ordeals. But when I was on the point of putting my resolve into execution, my courage failed me; for life is very precious. I clung instinctively to the hope of a speedy rescue, and a plan to protect myself from the serpent began to form in my mind.

I collected some thick planks of wood and fastened them together into a coffin-shaped box, complete with lid. When evening came I shut myself in, shielded on all sides by the strong boards. By and by the snake approached and circled round me, writhing and squirming. All night long its dreadful hissing sounded in my ears, but with the approach of morning it turned away and vanished among the undergrowth.

When the sun rose I came out of my shelter and cautiously made my way across the island. As I reached the shore, what should I see but a ship sailing far off upon the vast expanse of water!

At once I tore off a great branch from a tree, and, yelling at the top of my voice, waved it frantically above my head. The crew must have instantly observed my signal, for, to my great joy, the ship suddenly turned off its course and headed for the island.

When I came aboard the captain gave me clothes to cover my nakedness and offered me food and drink. Little by little I regained my strength, and after a few days of rest became my old self again. I rendered thanks to Allah for rescuing me from my ordeal, and soon my past sufferings were no more than half-forgotten dreams.

Aided by a prosperous wind, we voyaged many days and nights and at length came to the Isle of Salahiyah. Here the captain cast anchor, and the merchants landed with their goods to trade with the people of the island. Whilst I was standing idly by, watching the busy scene, the captain of our ship came up to me, saying: 'Listen, my friend. You say you are a penniless stranger who has suffered much at sea. I will make you an offer which, I trust, will be greatly to your advantage. A few years ago I carried in my ship a merchant who, alas, was left behind upon a desert island. No news has since been heard of him, and no one knows whether he is alive or dead. Take his goods and trade with them, and a share of the profit shall be yours. The remainder of the money I will take back to the merchant's family in Baghdad.'

I thanked the captain with all my heart. He ordered the crew to unload the merchandise and called the ship's clerk to enter up the bales in his register.

'Whose property are they?' inquired the clerk.

'The owner's name was Sindbad,' replied the captain. 'But henceforth they will be in charge of this passenger.'

A cry of astonishment escaped my lips and I at once recognized him as the captain of the ship in which I had sailed on my second voyage.

'Why!' I exclaimed. 'I am Sindbad, that very merchant

who many years ago was left behind on the Island of the Roc. I fell asleep beside a spring and awoke to find that the ship had gone. The merchants who saw me on the Diamond Mountains and heard my adventure will bear witness that I am indeed Sindbad.'

On hearing mention of the Diamond Mountains, one of the merchants, who by this time had gathered round us, came forward and, peering closely into my face, suddenly turned to his friends, crying: 'By Allah, not one of you would believe the wonder which I once witnessed on the Diamond Mountains, when a man was carried up from the valley by a mighty vulture! This is he; Sindbad the Sailor, the very one who presented me with those rare diamonds!'

The captain questioned me about the contents of my bales, and I readily gave him a precise description. I also reminded him of a certain incident which had occurred in the course of our voyage. He now recognized me and, taking me in his arms, congratulated me, saying: 'Praise be to Him who has brought us together again and granted the restitution of all your goods!'

My merchandise was brought ashore, and I sold it forthwith at a substantial profit. Then we set sail and after a few days came to the land of Sind, where we also traded profitably.

In those Indian waters I witnessed many prodigies. I saw a sea-monster which resembled a cow and another with a head like a donkey's. I also saw a bird which hatches from a sea-shell and remains throughout its life floating on the water.

From Sind we set sail again and, after voyaging many

days and nights, came at length with Allah's help to Basrah. I stayed there but a few days, and then voyaged upstream to Baghdad, where I was jubilantly welcomed by my friends and kinsmen. I bestowed alms upon the poor and gave generously to widows and orphans, for I had returned from this voyage richer than ever before.

Tomorrow, my friends, if Allah wills, I shall recount to you the tale of my fourth voyage, which you shall find even more extraordinary than the tales I have already related.

When the evening feast was ended, Sindbad the Sailor gave Sindbad the Porter a hundred pieces of gold, and the company took leave of their host and departed, marvelling at the wonders they had heard.

Next morning the porter returned, and when the other guests had assembled, Sindbad the Sailor began:

The Fourth Voyage of Sindbad the Sailor

The jovial and extravagant life which I led after my return did not cause me to forget the delights and benefits of travel in distant lands; and my thirst for seeing the world, despite the perils I had encountered, continued as violent as ever. My restless soul at length yielded to the call of the sea and, after making preparations for a long voyage, I set sail with merchandise from Basrah, together with some eminent merchants of that city.

Blessed with a favouring wind, we sped upon the foamy highways of the sea, trading from port to port and from island to island. One day, however, a howling gale suddenly sprang up in mid ocean, rolling against our ship massive waves as high as mountains. The captain at once ordered the crew to cast anchor, and we all fell on our knees in prayer and lamentation. A furious squall tore the sails to ribbons and snapped the mast in two; then a giant wave came hurtling down upon us from above, shattering our vessel and tossing us all into the raging sea.

With Allah's help, I clung fast to a floating beam, and bestriding it firmly, fought the downrush of the waves with those of my companions who had managed to reach it also. Now paddling with our hands and feet, now swept by wind and current, we were at length thrown, half-dead with cold and exhaustion, on the shore of an island.

We lay down upon the sand and fell asleep. Next morning we rose and, striking inland, came after a few hours in sight of a lofty building among the trees. As we drew nearer, a number of naked and wild-looking men emerged from the door, and without a word took hold of my companions and myself and led us into the building, where we saw their King seated upon a throne.

The King bade us sit down, and presently his servants set before us dishes of such meats as we had never seen before in all our lives. My famished companions ate ravenously; but my stomach revolted at the sight of this food and, in spite of my hunger, I could not eat a single mouthful. As things turned out, however, my abstinence saved my life. For as soon as they had swallowed a few morsels my comrades began to lose their intelligence and to act like gluttonous maniacs, so that after a few hours of incessant guzzling they were little better than savages.

Whilst my companions were thus feeding, the naked men brought in a vessel filled with a strange ointment, with which they anointed their victims' bodies. The change my companions suffered was astonishing; their eyes sank into their heads and their bellies grew horribly distended, so that the more they swelled the more insatiable their appetites became.

My horror at this spectacle knew no bounds, especially when I soon discovered that our captors were cannibals who fattened their victims in this way before slaughtering them. The King feasted every day on a roasted stranger; his men preferred their diet raw.

When my transformed companions had thus been robbed entirely of all their human faculties, they were committed to the charge of a herdsman, who led them out every day to pasture in the meadows. I myself was reduced to a shadow by hunger and fear and my skin shrivelled upon my bones. Therefore the savages lost all interest in me and no longer cared even to watch my movements.

One day I slipped out of my captors' dwelling and made off across the island. On reaching the distant grass-lands I met the herdsman with his once-human charges. But instead of pursuing me or ordering me to return he appeared to take pity on my helpless condition, and pointing to his right made signs to me which seemed to say: 'Go this way: have no fear.'

I ran on and on across the rolling plains in the direction

he indicated. When evening came I ate a scanty meal of roots and herbs and lay down to rest upon the grass; but fear of the cannibals had robbed me of all desire to sleep, and at midnight I rose again and trudged painfully on.

Thus I journeyed for seven days and nights, and on the morning of the eighth day came at last to the opposite side of the island, where I could faintly discern human figures in the distance. Drawing nearer, I rejoiced to find that they were a party of peasants gathering pepper in a field.

They crowded round me, and speaking in my own language inquired who I was and whence I had come. In reply I recounted the story of my misfortunes, and they were all amazed at my adventure. They congratulated me on my escape and, after offering me food and water, allowed me to rest till evening. When their day's work was done, they took me with them in a boat to their capital, which was in a neighbouring island.

There I was presented to their King, who received me kindly and listened in astonishment to my story. I found their city prosperous and densely populated, abounding in markets and well-stocked shops, and filled with the bustle of commercial activity. The people, both rich and poor, possessed the rarest thoroughbred horses; but I was bewildered to see them ride their steeds bare-backed.

In my next audience with the King I ventured to express my surprise at his subjects' ignorance of the use of saddles and stirrups. 'My noble master,' I remarked, 'why is it that no one in this island uses a saddle? It makes both for the comfort of the rider and his mastery over his horse.'

'What may that be?' he asked, somewhat puzzled. 'I have never seen a saddle in all my life.'

'Pray allow me to make one for you,' I replied, 'that you may try it and find how comfortable and useful it can be.'

The King was pleased at my offer. At once I sought out a skilful carpenter and instructed him to make a wooden frame for a saddle of my own design; then I taught a blacksmith to forge a bit and a pair of stirrups. I fitted out the frame with a padding of wool and leather and furnished it with a girth and tassels. When all was ready, I chose the finest of the royal horses, saddled and bridled it, and led it before the King.

The King was highly delighted with the splendour and usefulness of his horse's novel equipment, and in reward bestowed on me precious gifts and a large sum of money.

When his Vizier saw the saddle he begged me to make one for him. I did so; and it was not long before every courtier and noble in the kingdom became the owner of a handsome saddle.

My skill soon made me the richest man in the island. The King conferred upon me many honours and I became a trusted courtier. One day, as we sat conversing together in his palace, he said: 'You must know, Sindbad, that we have grown to love you like a brother. Indeed, our regard for you is such that we cannot bear the thought that you might some day leave our kingdom. Therefore we will ask you a favour, which we hope you will not refuse.'

'Allah forbid,' I replied, 'that I should refuse you anything, your majesty.'

'We wish you to marry a beautiful girl who has been brought up in our court,' he said. 'She is intelligent and wealthy, and will make you an excellent wife. I trust that you will settle down happily with her in this city for the rest of your days. Do not refuse me this, I pray you.'

I was deeply embarrassed and did not know what to answer.

'Why do you not speak, my son?' he asked.

'Your majesty,' I faltered, 'I am in duty bound to obey you.'

The King sent at once for a cadi and witnesses and I was married that day to a rich woman of noble lineage. The King gave us a magnificent palace and assigned to us a retinue of slaves and servants.

We lived happily and contentedly together, although in my heart of hearts I never ceased to cherish a longing to return home – together with my wife; for I loved her dearly. But, alas, no mortal can control his destiny or trifle with the decrees of Fate.

One day death took my neighbour's wife to eternal rest, and, as he was one of my closest friends, I visited him at his house to offer my condolence. Finding him overcome with grief, I tried to comfort him, saying: 'Have patience, my friend. Allah in His great bounty may soon give you another wife as loving and as worthy as the one He has taken from you. May He lighten your sorrow and prolong your years!'

But he never raised his eyes from the ground.

'Alas!' he sighed. 'How can you wish me a long life when I have but a few hours to live?'

'Take heart, my friend,' I said, 'why do you speak of

34

death when, thank Allah, you are in perfect health, sound in mind and body?'

'In a few hours,' he replied, 'I shall be consigned to the earth with the body of my wife. It is an ancient custom in this country that when a wife dies her husband is buried with her, and if he should die first his wife is buried with him: both must leave this world together.'

'By Allah,' I cried in horror, 'this is a most barbarous custom! No civilized people could ever tolerate such monstrous cruelty!'

Whilst we were talking, my neighbour's friends and kinsfolk, together with a large crowd, came into the house and began to condole with him upon his wife's and his own impending death. Presently the funeral preparations were completed; the woman's body was laid in a coffin, and a long procession of mourners, headed by the husband, formed outside the house. And we all set out for the burial ground.

The procession halted at the foot of a steep mound overlooking the sea, where a stone was rolled away from the mouth of a deep pit, and into this pit the corpse was thrown. Next the mourners laid hold of my friend and lowered him by a long rope, together with seven loaves of bread and a pitcher of water. Then the stone was rolled back and we all returned to the city.

I hastened with a heavy heart to the King's palace, and when I was admitted to his presence I fell on my knees before him, crying: 'My noble master, I have visited many far countries and lived amongst all manner of men, but in all my life I have never seen or heard of anything so barbarous as your custom of burying the living with the dead. Are strangers, too, subject to this law, your majesty?'

'Certainly they are,' he replied. 'They must be interred with their dead wives. It is a time-hallowed custom to which all must submit.'

At this reply I felt as though my gall-bladder would burst open. I ran in haste to my own house, dreading lest my wife should have died since I last saw her. Finding her in perfect health, I comforted myself as best I could with the thought that I might one day find means of returning to my own country, or even die before my wife.

But Allah ordained otherwise. Soon afterwards my wife was stricken with an illness and in a few days surrendered her soul to the Merciful.

The King and all his courtiers came to my house to comfort me. The body of my wife was perfumed and arrayed in fine robes and rich ornaments. And when all was ready for the burial I was led behind the bier, at the head of a long procession.

When we came to the mound, the stone was lifted from the mouth of the pit and the body of my wife thrown in; then the mourners gathered round to bid me farewell, paying no heed to my protests and entreaties. They bound me with a long rope and lowered me into the pit, together with the customary loaves and pitcher of water. Then they rolled back the stone and went their way.

When I touched the bottom of the pit I found myself in a vast cavern filled with skeletons and reeking with the foul stench of decaying corpses. I threw myself upon the earth, crying: 'You deserve this fate, Sindbad! Here you have come to pay the last penalty for your avarice, your insatiable greed! What need had you to marry in this island? Would that you had died on the bare mountains or perished in the merciless sea!'

Tormented by the vision of a protracted death, I lay in an agony of despair for many hours. At length, feeling the effects of thirst and hunger, I unfastened the loaves and the pitcher of water and ate and drank sparingly. Then I lay in a corner which I had carefully cleared of bones.

For several days I languished in that charnel cave, and at length the time came when my provisions were exhausted. As I lay down, commending myself to Allah and waiting for my approaching end, the covering of the pit was suddenly lifted and there appeared at its mouth a crowd of mourners, who presently lowered into the cavern a dead man accompanied by his screaming wife, together with seven loaves and a pitcher of water.

As soon as the stone was rolled back I rose and, snatching up a leg-bone from one of the skeletons, sprang upon the woman and dealt her a violent blow upon the head, so that she fell down lifeless upon the instant. Then I stole her provisions, which kept me alive for several days longer. When these in turn were finished, the stone was once again rolled away from the pit and a man lowered in with his dead wife. He, too, met the same end as the unfortunate woman before him.

In this way I lived on for many weeks, killing every newcomer and eating his food. One day, as I was sleeping in my accustomed place, I was awakened by a sound of movement near by. At once I sprang to my feet, and picking up my weapon followed the noise until I could faintly discern the form of some animal scurrying before me. As I pressed forward in pursuit of the strange intruder, stumbling in the dark over the bones and corpses, I suddenly made out at the far side of the cavern a tremulous speck of light which grew larger and brighter as I advanced towards it. When I had reached the end of the cave the fleeing animal leapt through the light and disappeared. To my inexpressible joy, I realized that I had come upon a tunnel which the wild beasts, attracted by the carrion in the cave, had burrowed from the other side of the mound. I scrambled into this tunnel, crawling on all fours, and soon found myself at the foot of a high cliff, beneath the open sky.

I fell upon my knees in prayer and thanked the Almighty for my salvation. The warm and wholesome air breathed new life into my veins, and I rejoiced to gaze upon the loveliness of earth and sky.

Fortified with hope and courage, I made my way back into the cave and brought out the store of food which I had laid aside during my sojourn there. I also gathered up all the jewels, pearls, and precious ornaments that I could find upon the corpses, and, tying them in the shrouds and garments of the dead, carried the bundles to the seashore.

I remained there several days, surveying the horizon from morning till night. One day, as I was sitting beneath a rock praying for a speedy rescue, I saw a sail far off upon the ocean. I hoisted a winding-sheet on my staff and waved it frantically as I ran up and down the beach.

The crew observed my signal, and a boat was promptly sent off to fetch me.

'How did you find your way to this wild region?' asked the captain in astonishment. 'I have never seen a living man on this desolate spot in all the days of my life.'

'Sir,' I replied, 'I was shipwrecked off this shore many days ago. These bales are the remnants of my goods which I managed to save.' And I kept the truth from him, lest there be some on board who were citizens of that island.

Then I took out a rare pearl from one of my packages and offered it to him. 'Pray accept this,' I said, 'as a token of my gratitude to you for saving my life.'

But the captain politely refused the gift. 'It is not our custom,' he said, 'to accept payment for a good deed. We have rescued many a shipwrecked voyager, fed him and clothed him and finally set him ashore with a little present of our own besides. Allah alone is the giver of rewards.'

I thanked him with all my heart and called down blessings upon him.

Then the ship resumed its voyage. And, as we sailed from island to island and from sea to sea, I rejoiced at the prospect of seeing my native land again. At times, however, a memory of my sojourn with the dead would come back to me and I would be beside myself with terror.

At length, by the grace of Allah, we arrived safely in Basrah. I stayed a few days in that town, and then proceeded up the river to Baghdad. Loaded with treasure, I hastened to my own house, where I was rapturously welcomed by my friends and kinsfolk. I sold for a fabulous sum the precious stones I had brought back from that barbarous city, and gave lavish alms to widows and orphans.

That is the story of my fourth voyage. Tomorrow, if Allah wills, I shall recount to you the adventures of my fifth voyage.

When the evening feast was over, Sindbad the Sailor gave Sindbad the Porter a hundred pieces of gold, and the company took leave of their host and departed, marvelling at all they had heard. Next morning the porter returned, and when the other guests had assembled, Sindbad the Sailor began:

The Fifth Voyage of Sindbad the Sailor

Know, my friends, that the idle and indulgent life which I led after my return soon made me forget the suffering I had endured in the Land of the Cannibals and in the Cavern of the Dead. I remembered only the pleasures of adventure and the considerable gains which my travels had earned me, and once again longed to sail new seas and explore new lands. I equipped myself with commodities suitable for ready sale in foreign countries and, packing them in bales, took them to Basrah.

One day, as I was walking along the wharf, I saw a newly built ship with tall masts and fine new sails which at once caught my fancy. I bought her outright, and embarked in her my slaves and merchandise. Then I hired an experienced captain and a well-trained crew, and accepted as passengers several other merchants who offered to pay their fares beforehand.

Blessed with a favourable wind, we voyaged many days and nights, trading from sea to sea and from shore to shore, and at length came to a desert island where we caught sight of a solitary white dome, half-buried in the sand. This I recognized at once as a roc's egg; and the passengers begged leave to land, so that they might go near and gaze upon this prodigy.

As ill luck would have it, however, the light-hearted merchants found no better sport than to throw great stones at the egg. When the shell was broken, the passengers, who were determined to have a feast, dragged out the young bird and cut it up in pieces. Then they returned on board to tell me of their adventure.

I was filled with horror and cried: 'We are lost! The parent birds will now pursue our ship with implacable rage and destroy us all!'

Scarcely had I finished speaking when the sun was suddenly hidden from our view as by a great cloud and the world grew dark around us as the rocs came flying home. On finding their egg broken and their offspring destroyed, the birds uttered deafening cries; they took to the air again, and in a twinkling vanished from sight.

'All aboard, quickly!' I exclaimed. 'We must at once flee from this island!'

The captain weighed anchor and with all speed we sailed off towards the open sea. But before long the world grew dark again, and in the ominous twilight we could see the gigantic birds hovering high overhead, each carrying in its talons an enormous rock. When they were directly above us, one of them let fall its missile, which narrowly missed the ship and made such a chasm in the ocean that for a moment we could see the sandy bottom. The waves rose mountain-high, tossing us up and down. Presently the other bird dropped its rock, which hit the stern and sent the rudder flying into twenty pieces. Those of us who were not crushed to death were hurled into the sea and swallowed up by the giant waves.

Through the grace of Allah I managed to cling to a floating piece of wreckage. Sitting astride this, I paddled with my feet, and, aided by wind and current, at length reached the shore of an island.

I threw myself upon the sand and lay down awhile to recover my breath. Then I rose and wandered about the island, which was as beautiful as one of the gardens of Eden. The air was filled with the singing of birds, and wherever I turned my eyes I saw trees loaded with luscious fruit and crystal brooks meandering among banks of flowers. I refreshed myself with the fruit and water, and when evening came lay down upon the grass.

Early next morning I rose and set off to explore this solitary garden. After a long stroll among the trees I came to a rivulet where, to my astonishment, I saw, seated upon the bank, a decrepit old man cloaked in a mantle of leaves.

Taking him for a shipwrecked mariner like myself, I went up to him and wished him peace; but he replied only by a mournful nod. I asked him what luckless accident had cast him in that place, but instead of answering he entreated me with signs to take him upon my shoulders and carry him across the brook. I readily bent down and, lifting him upon my back, waded through the stream. When I reached the opposite bank I stooped again for him to get off; but instead of alighting the old wretch powerfully threw his legs, which I now saw were covered with a rough black skin like a buffalo's, round my neck and crossed them tightly over my chest. Seized with fear, I desperately tried to shake him off, but the monster pressed his thighs tighter and tighter round my throat until I could no longer breathe. The world darkened before my eyes and with a choking cry I fell senseless to the ground.

When I came to myself I found the old monster still crouching upon my shoulders, although he had now sufficiently relaxed his hold to allow me to breathe. As soon as he saw that I had recovered my senses he pushed one foot against my belly and, violently kicking my side with the other, forced me to rise and walk under some trees. He leisurely plucked the fruits and ate them, and every time I stopped against his will or failed to do his bidding he kicked me hard, so that I had no choice but to obey him. All day long he remained seated upon my shoulders, and I was no better than a captive slave; at night he made me lie down with him, never for one moment loosening his hold round my neck. Next morning he roused me with a kick and ordered me to carry him among the trees.

Thus he stayed rooted upon my back, discharging his natural filth upon me, and driving me relentlessly on from glade to glade. I cursed the charitable impulse which prompted me to help him, and longed for death to deliver me from my evil plight.

After many weeks of abject servitude I chanced one day to come upon a field where gourds were growing in abundance. Under one of the trees I found a large gourd which was sun-dried and empty. I picked it up and, after cleaning it thoroughly, squeezed into it the juice of several bunches of grapes; then, carefully stopping the hole which I had cut into its shell, left it in the sun to ferment.

When I returned with the old man a few days afterwards, I found the gourd filled with the purest wine. The drink gave me fresh vigour, and I presently began to feel so light and gay that I went tripping merrily among the trees, scarcely aware of my loathsome burden.

Perceiving the effect of the wine, my captor asked me to let him taste it. I did not dare to refuse. He took the gourd from my hand, and raising it to his lips gulped down the liquor to the dregs. When he was overcome with the wine, he began to sway from side to side and his legs gradually relaxed their clasp round my neck. With one violent jerk of my shoulders I hurled him to the ground, where he lay motionless. Then I quickly picked up a great stone from among the trees and, falling upon the old fiend with all my strength, crushed his skull to pieces and mingled his flesh with his blood. That was the end of my tormentor: may Allah have no mercy upon him!

Overjoyed at my new freedom, I roamed the island for many weeks, eating of its fruit and drinking from its springs. One day, however, as I sat on the shore musing

on the vicissitudes of my life and recalling memories of
my native land, I saw to my great joy a sail heading
towards the island. On reaching the beach the vessel
anchored, and the passengers went ashore to fill their
pitchers with water.

I ran in haste to meet them. They were greatly astonished to see me and gathered round, inquiring who
I was and whence I had come. I recounted to them all
that had befallen me since my arrival, and they replied:
'It is a marvel that you have escaped from that fiend; for
you must know that the monster who had crouched
upon your shoulders was none other than the Old Man
of the Sea. You are the first ever to escape alive from his
clutches. Praise be to Allah for your deliverance!'

They took me to their ship, where the captain received
me kindly and listened with astonishment to my adventure. Then we set sail, and after voyaging many days and
nights cast anchor in the harbour of a city perched on a
high cliff, which is known among travellers as the City
of Apes on account of the hosts of monkeys that infest
it by night.

I went ashore with one of the merchants from the
ship and wandered about the town in search of some
employment. We soon fell in with a crowd of men
proceeding to the gates of the city with sacks of pebbles
on their shoulders. At the sight of these men my friend
the merchant gave me a large cotton bag, saying: 'Fill
this with pebbles and follow these people into the forest.
Do exactly as they do, and thus you will earn your
livelihood.'

Following his instructions, I filled the sack with

pebbles and joined the crowd. The merchant recommended me to them, saying: 'Here is a shipwrecked stranger; teach him to earn his bread and Allah will reward you.'

When we had marched a great distance from the city we came to a vast valley, covered with coconut-trees so straight and tall that no man could ever climb them. Drawing nearer, I saw among the trees innumerable monkeys, which fled at our approach and swiftly climbed up to the fruit-laden branches.

Here my companions set down their bags and began to pelt the apes with pebbles; and I did the same. The furious beasts retaliated by pelting us with coconuts, and these we gathered up and put into our sacks. When they were full we returned to the city and sold the nuts in the market-place.

Thenceforth I went out every day to the forest with the coconut hunters and traded profitably with the fruit. When I had saved enough money for my homeward voyage I took leave of my friend the merchant and embarked in a vessel bound for Basrah, taking with me a large cargo of coconuts and other produce of that city.

In the course of our voyage we stopped at many heathen islands, where I sold some of my coconuts at a substantial profit and exchanged others for cinnamon, pepper, and Chinese and Comarin aloes. On reaching the Sea of Pearls I engaged the services of several divers; and in a short time brought up a large quantity of priceless pearls.

After that we again set sail and, voyaging many days and nights, at length safely arrived in Basrah. I spent but a few days in that town, and then, loaded with treasure, set out for Baghdad. I rejoiced to be back in my native city, and hastening to my old street, entered my own house, where all my friends and kinsmen forgathered to greet me. I gave them gold and countless presents, and distributed a large sum in charity among the widows and orphans.

That is the story of my fifth voyage. Tomorrow, my friends, if Allah wills, I shall recount to you the tale of my sixth voyage.

When the evening feast was ended, Sindbad the Sailor gave Sindbad the Porter a hundred pieces of gold, and the company departed, marvelling at all they had heard.

Next morning the porter returned and, when the other guests had arrived, Sindbad the Sailor began:

The Sixth Voyage of Sindbad the Sailor

I was one day reclining at my ease in the comfort and felicity of a serene life, when a band of merchants who had just returned from abroad called at my house to give me news of foreign lands. The sight of these travellers recalled to my mind how great was the joy of returning from a far journey to be united with friends and kinsmen after a prolonged absence; and soon afterwards I made preparations for another voyage and set sail with a rich cargo from Basrah.

We voyaged leisurely many days and nights, buying and selling wherever the ship anchored and exploring the unfamiliar places at which we called. One day, how-ever, as we were sailing in mid ocean, we suddenly heard the captain of our ship burst out in a loud lament. He beat himself about the face, tore at his beard, and hurled his turban on the deck. We gathered round him, inquiring the cause of his violent grief.

'Alas, we are lost!' he cried. 'The ship has been driven off its course into an unknown ocean, where nothing can save us from final wreck but Allah's mercy. Let us pray to Him!'

Then, quickly rising, the captain climbed the mast to trim the sails, while the passengers fell on their knees weeping and bidding each other farewell. Scarcely had he reached the top when a violent gale arose, sweeping us swiftly along and dashing the ship against a craggy shore at the foot of a high mountain. At once the vessel split into pieces and we were all flung into the raging sea. Some were drowned outright, while others, like myself, managed to escape by clinging to the jutting rocks.

We found scattered all along the shore the remains of other wrecks, and the sands were strewn with countless bales from which rare merchandise and costly ornaments had broken loose. I wandered among these treasures for many hours, and then, winding my way through the rocks, suddenly came upon a river which flowed from a gorge in the mountain. I followed its course with my eyes and was surprised to find that instead of running into the sea, the river plunged into a vast rocky cavern and disappeared. The banks were covered with glittering jewels, and the bed was studded with myriads of rubies, emeralds, and other precious stones; so that the entire river blazed with a dazzling light. The rarest Chinese and Comarin aloes grew on the adjacent steeps, and liquid amber trickled down the rocks onto the beach below. Great whales would come out of the sea and drink of this amber; but, their bellies being gradually heated, they would at length disgorge it upon the surface of the water. There it would crystallize and, after changing its colour and other properties, would finally be washed ashore, its rich perfume scenting the entire region.

Those of us who had escaped drowning lay in a sorrowful plight upon the shore, counting the days as they dragged by and waiting for the approach of death. One by one my companions died as they came to the end of their provisions, and we who were left washed the dead and wrapped them in winding sheets made from the fabrics scattered on the shore, and buried them. Then my friends were stricken with a sickness of the belly, caused by the humid air, to which they all succumbed; and I had the melancholy task of burying with my own hands the last of my companions.

Realizing that death was at hand, I threw myself upon the earth, wailing: 'Would that I had died before my friends! There would at least have remained good comrades who would have washed my body and given it a decent burial! There is no strength or help save in Allah!'

At length I rose and dug a deep grave by the sea, thinking to myself: 'When I sense the approach of death I will lie here and die in my grave. In time the wind will bury me with sand.' And as I thus prepared to meet my end, I cursed myself for venturing yet again upon the perils of the sea after having suffered so many misfortunes in my past voyages. 'Why,' I cried in my despair, 'oh why were you not content to remain safe and happy in Baghdad? Had you not enough riches to last you twice a lifetime?'

Lost in these reflections, I wandered to the banks of the river, and as I watched it disappear into the cavern I struck upon a plan. 'By Allah,' I thought, 'this river must have both a beginning and an end. If it enters the mountain on this side it must surely emerge into daylight again; and if I can but follow its course in some vessel, the current may at last bring me to some inhabited land. If I am destined to survive this peril, Allah will guide me to safety; if I perish, it will not be worse than the dismal fate which awaits me here.'

Emboldened by these thoughts, I collected some large branches of Chinese and Comarin aloes and, laying these on some planks from the wrecked vessels, bound them with strong cables into a raft. This I loaded with sacks of rubies, pearls, and other stones, as well as several bales of the choicest ambergris; then, commending myself to Allah, I launched the raft upon the water and jumped aboard.

The current carried me swiftly along, and I soon found myself enveloped in the brooding darkness of the cavern. My raft began to bump violently against the ragged sides, while the passage grew smaller and narrower until I was compelled to lie flat upon my belly for fear of striking my head. Very soon I wished I could return to the open shore, but the current became faster and faster as the river swept headlong down its precipitous bed, and

I resigned myself to certain death. At length, overcome by terror and exertion, I sank into a death-like sleep.

I cannot tell how long I slept, but when I awoke I found myself lying on my raft close to the river bank, beneath the open sky. The river was flowing gently through a stretch of pleasant meadowland, and on the bank stood many Indians and Abyssinians.

As soon as these men saw that I was awake, they gathered about me, asking questions in a language I did not understand. Presently one of their number came forward and greeted me in Arabic.

'Who may you be?' he asked, 'and whence have you come? We were working in our fields when we saw you drifting down the river. We fastened your raft to this bank and, not wishing to disturb your slumbers, left you here in safety. But tell us, what accident has cast you upon this river, which takes its perilous course from beneath that mountain?'

I begged him first to give me some food, and promised to answer all their questions after I had eaten. They instantly brought me a variety of meats, and when I had regained my strength a little, I recounted to them all that had befallen me since my shipwreck. They marvelled at my miraculous escape, and said: 'We must take you to our King, so that you may yourself tell him of your adventure.'

Thereupon they led me to their city, carrying my raft with all its contents upon their shoulders. The King received me courteously and, after listening in profound astonishment to my story, congratulated me heartily on my escape. Then, opening my treasures in his presence,

I laid out at his feet a priceless choice of emeralds, pearls, and rubies. In return he conferred upon me the highest honours of the kingdom, and invited me to stay as his guest at the palace.

Thus I rose rapidly in the King's favour, and soon became a trusted courtier. One day he questioned me about my country and its far-famed Caliph. I praised the wisdom, piety, and benevolence of Haroun Al-Rashid, and spoke at length of his glorious deeds. The King was deeply impressed by my account. 'This monarch,' he said, 'must indeed be illustrious. We desire to send him a present worthy of his greatness, and appoint you the bearer of it.'

'I hear and obey,' I replied. 'I will gladly deliver your gift to the Prince of the Faithful, and will inform him that in your majesty he has a worthy ally and a trusted friend.'

The King gave orders that a magnificent present be prepared and commissioned a new vessel for the voyage. When all was ready for departure I presented myself at the royal palace and, thanking the King for the many favours he had shown me, took leave of him and of the officers of his court.

Then I set sail, and voyaging many days and nights at length safely arrived in Basrah. I hastened to Baghdad with the royal gift, and when I had been admitted to the Caliph's presence I kissed the ground before him and told him of my mission. Al-Rashid marvelled greatly at my adventure and gave orders that the story be inscribed on parchment in letters of gold, so that it might be preserved among the treasures of the kingdom.

Leaving his court, I hastened to my old street and,

entering my own house, rejoiced to meet my friends and kinsfolk. I gave them gold and costly presents, and distributed lavish alms among the poor of the city.

Such is the story of my sixth voyage. Tomorrow, my friends, I shall recount to you the tale of my seventh and last voyage.

When the evening feast was ended, Sindbad the Sailor gave Sindbad the Porter a hundred pieces of gold, and the guests departed, marvelling at all they had heard.

Next morning the porter returned and, when the other guests had assembled, Sindbad the Sailor began:

The Last Voyage of Sindbad the Sailor

For many years after my return I lived joyfully in Baghdad, feasting and carousing with my boon companions and revelling away the riches which my far-flung travels had earned me. But though I was now past the prime of life, my untamed spirit rebelled against my declining years, and I once again longed to see the world and travel in the lands of men. I made preparations for a long voyage and, boarding a good ship in company with some eminent merchants, set sail from Basrah with a fair wind and a rich cargo.

We voyaged peacefully for many weeks, but one day, whilst we were sailing in the China Sea, a violent tempest struck our ship, drenching us with torrents of rain. We hastily covered our bales with canvas to protect them from the wet and fervently prayed to Allah to save us from the fury of the sea, while the captain, rolling up his sleeves and tucking the skirts of his robes into his belt, climbed the mast and from the top scanned the horizon in all directions. Presently he climbed down again, all of a tremble with terror and, staring at us with an expression of blank despair, beat his face and plucked the hairs of his beard.

'Pray to Allah,' he cried, 'that He may save us from the peril into which we have fallen! Weep and say your farewells, for the treacherous wind has got the better of us and driven our ship into the world's farthermost ocean!'

Thereupon the captain opened one of his cabin chests and took from it a small cotton bag filled with an ashlike powder. He sprinkled some water over the powder and, after waiting a little, inhaled it into his nostrils; then, opening a little book, he intoned aloud some strange incantations and at length turned to us, crying: 'Know that we are now approaching the Realm of Kings, the very land where our master Solomon son of David (may peace be upon him!) lies buried. Serpents of prodigious size swarm about that coast, and the sea is filled with giant whales which can swallow vessels whole. Farewell, my friends; and may Allah have mercy upon us all!'

Scarcely had the captain uttered these words when suddenly the ship was tossed high up in the air and then flung down into the sea, while an ear-splitting cry, more terrible than thunder, boomed through the swelling ocean. Terror seized our hearts as we saw a gigantic whale, as massive as a mountain, rushing swiftly towards us, followed by another no less huge, and a third greater than the two put together. This last monster bounded from the surging billows and, opening wide its enormous mouth, seized in its jaws the ship with all that was in it. I hastily ran to the edge of the tilting deck and, casting off my clothes, leapt into the sea just before the whale swallowed up the ship and disappeared beneath the foam with its two companions.

With Allah's help I clung to a piece of timber which had fallen from the lost vessel and, contending with the mighty waves for two days and nights, was at length cast on an island covered with fruit-trees and watered by many streams. After refreshing myself I wandered aimlessly about, and soon came to a fast-flowing river which rolled its waters towards the interior of the island. As I stood upon the bank I hit upon the idea of building a raft and allowing myself to be carried down by the current, as I had done in my last voyage. 'If I succeed in saving myself this time,' I said, 'all will be well with me and I solemnly vow never in all my life to let the mere thought of voyaging cross my mind again. If I fail, I shall at last find rest from all the toils and tribulations which my incorrigible folly has earned me.'

I cut down several branches from an exotic tree which I had never seen before and bound them together into a raft with the stems of some creeping plants. I loaded the raft with a large quantity of fruit and, commending myself to Allah, pushed off down the river.

For three days and nights I was hurried swiftly along by the current, until, overcome by dizziness, I sank into a dead faint. When I recovered consciousness I found myself heading towards a fearful precipice, down which

the waters of the river were tumbling in a mighty catar-
act. I clung with all my strength to the branches of the
raft and, resigning myself to my fate, prayed silently for
a merciful end. When I had reached the very edge of the
precipice, however, I suddenly felt the raft halted upon
the water and found myself caught in a net which a
crowd of men had thrown from the bank. My raft was
quickly hauled to land, and I was released from the net
half dead with terror and exhaustion.

As I lay upon the mud, I gradually became aware of
a venerable old man who was bending over me. He
wrapped me in warm garments and greeted me kindly;
and when my strength had returned a little he helped
me to rise and led me slowly to the baths of the city,
where I was washed with perfumed water. Then the
old man took me to his own house. He regaled me
sumptuously with excellent meats and wines and, when
the feast was ended, his slaves washed my hands and
wiped them with napkins of the rarest silk. My host
conducted me to a noble chamber and left me alone,
after assigning several of his slaves to my service.

The kind old man entertained me in this fashion for
three days. When I had completely recovered, he visited
me in my chamber and sat conversing with me for an
hour. Just before leaving my room, however, he turned
to me and said: 'If you wish to sell your merchandise,
my friend, I will gladly come down with you to the
market-place.'

I was greatly puzzled at these words and did not know
what to answer, as I had been cast utterly naked in that
city.

'Do not be troubled over your goods, my son,' went on the old man. 'If we receive a good offer, we will sell them outright; if not, I will keep them for you in my own storehouse until they fetch a better price.'

Concealing my perplexity, I replied: 'I am willing to do whatever you advise.' With this I rose and went out with him to the market-place.

There I saw an excited crowd admiring an object on the ground with exclamations of enthusiastic praise. Pushing my way through the gesticulating merchants, I was astonished to find the centre of attention to be none other than the raft aboard which I had sailed down the river. And presently the old man ordered a broker to begin the auction.

'Who will make the first bid for this rare sandalwood?' began the broker.

'A hundred dinars!' cried one of the merchants.

'A thousand!' shouted another.

'Eleven hundred!' exclaimed my host.

'Agreed!' I cried.

Upon this the old man ordered his slaves to carry the wood to his store and walked back with me to his house, where he paid me eleven hundred pieces of gold locked in an iron coffer.

One day, as we sat conversing together, the old man said: 'My son, pray grant me a favour.'

'With all my heart,' I replied.

'I am a very old man, and have not been blessed with a son,' went on my benefactor. 'Yet I have a young and beautiful daughter, who on my death will be sole mistress of my fortune. If you will have her for your wife, you will inherit my wealth and become chief of the merchants of this city.'

I readily consented to the sheikh's proposal. A sumptuous feast was held, a cadi and witnesses were called in, and I was married to the old man's daughter amidst great rejoicings. When the wedding guests had departed I was conducted to the bridal chamber, where I was allowed to see my wife for the first time. I found her incomparably beautiful, and rejoiced to see her decked with the rarest pearls and jewels.

My wife and I grew to love each other dearly, and we lived together in happiness and contentment. Not long afterwards my wife's father died, and I inherited all his possessions. His slaves became my slaves and his goods my goods, and the merchants of the city appointed me their chief in his place.

One day, however, I discovered that every year the people of that land experienced a wondrous change in their bodies. All the men grew wings upon their shoulders and for a whole day flew high up in the air, leaving their wives and children behind. Amazed at this prodigy, I importuned one of my friends to allow me to cling to him when he next took flight, and at length prevailed on him to let me try this novel adventure. When the long-awaited day arrived, I took tight hold of my friend's waist and was at once carried up swiftly in the air. We climbed higher and higher into the void until I could hear the angels in their choirs singing hymns to Allah under the vault of heaven. Moved with awe, I cried: 'Glory and praise eternal be to Allah, King of the Universe!'

Scarcely had I uttered these words when my winged carrier dropped headlong through the air and finally alighted on the top of a high mountain. There he threw me off his back and took to the air again, calling down curses on my head. Abandoned upon this desolate mountain, I lifted my hands in despair and cried: 'There is no strength or help save in Allah! Every time I escape from one ordeal I find myself in another as grievous. Surely I deserve all that befalls me!'

Whilst I was thus reflecting upon my plight, I saw two youths coming up towards me. Their faces shone with an unearthly beauty, and each held a staff of red gold in his hand. I at once rose to my feet, and, walking towards them, wished them peace. They returned my greeting courteously, and I inquired: 'Who are you, pray, and what object has brought you to this barren mountain?'

'We are worshippers of the True God,' they replied. With this, one of the youths pointed to a certain path upon the mountain and, handing me his staff, walked away with his companion.

Bewildered at these words, I set off in the direction he had indicated, leaning upon my gold staff as I walked. I had not gone far when I saw coming towards me the flyer who had so unceremoniously set me down upon the mountain. Determined to learn the reason of his displeasure, I went up to him and said gently: 'Is this how friends behave to friends?'

The winged man, who was now no longer angry, replied: 'Know that my fall was caused by your unfortunate mention of your god. The word has this effect upon us all, and this is why we never utter it.'

I assured my friend that I had meant no harm and promised to commit no such transgression in future. Then I begged him to carry me back to the city. He took me upon his shoulders and in a few moments set me down before my own house.

My wife was overjoyed at my return, and when I told her of my adventure, she said: 'We must no longer stay among these people. Know that they are the brothers of Satan and have no knowledge of the True God.'

'How then did your father dwell amongst them?' I asked.

'My father was of an alien race,' she replied. 'He shared none of their creeds, and he did not lead their life. As he is now dead, let us sell our possessions and leave this blasphemous city.'

Thereupon I resolved to return home. We sold our houses and other property, and hiring a vessel set sail with a rich cargo.

Aided by a favouring wind, we voyaged many days and nights and at length came to Basrah and thence to Baghdad, the City of Peace. I conveyed to my stores the valuables I had brought with me, and, taking my wife to my own house in my old street, rejoiced to meet my kinsfolk and my old companions. They told me that this voyage had kept me abroad for nearly twenty-seven years, and marvelled exceedingly at all that had befallen me.

I rendered deep thanks to Allah for bringing me safely back to my friends and kinsfolk, and solemnly vowed never to travel again by sea or land. Such, dear guests, was the last and longest of my voyages.

*

When the evening feast was ended, Sindbad the Sailor gave Sindbad the Porter a hundred pieces of gold, which he took with thanks and blessings and departed, marvelling at all he had heard.

The porter remained a constant visitor at the house of his illustrious friend, and the two lived in amity and peace until there came to them the Spoiler of worldly mansions, the Dark Steward of the graveyard; the Shadow which dissolves the bonds of friendship and ends alike all joys and all sorrows.

The Tale of Ma'aruf the Cobbler

Once upon a time there lived in the city of Cairo a poor and honest cobbler who earned his living by patching old shoes. His name was Ma'aruf.

He was married to a spiteful termagant called Fatimah, nicknamed by her neighbours 'The Shrew' on account of her sour disposition and scolding tongue. She used her husband with heartless cruelty, cursing him a thousand times a day and making his life a burden and a torment. Ma'aruf was a sensitive man, jealous of his good name, and in time he grew to fear her malice and dread her fiery temper. All his daily earnings he gladly spent on her, but if, by ill fortune, he returned home with an empty purse, she abused and scolded him, giving him no rest and making his night hideous as her scowl.

It happened one day that his wife came to Ma'aruf and said: 'See that you bring me a kunafah cake tonight, and let it be dripping with sweet honey.'

'May Allah send me good custom today,' replied the cobbler, 'and you shall gladly have one. At present I have not a single copper, but the bounty of Allah is great.'

'A fig for the bounty of Allah!' rejoined the shrew. 'If you do not bring me back a kunafah, dripping with sweet honey, I will make the night blacker for you than the fate which cast you into my hands!'

'Allah is merciful,' sighed Ma'aruf. Perplexed and

downcast, he left his house and went to open his shop, saying: 'O Allah, grant me this day the means to buy a honey-cake for my wife, that I may save myself from the spleen of that wicked woman!'

But, as ill luck would have it, no customer entered his shop that day and he did not earn enough even to buy a loaf of bread. Weary and sick at heart, he locked his shop and walked along the street. Presently he came to a pastry-cook's, and as he gazed upon the delicacies displayed in the window, his eyes filled with tears. Noticing his dejected countenance, the pastry-cook called out to him, saying: 'Why so sad, Ma'aruf? Come in, and tell me your trouble.'

When the cook had heard the cause of the cobbler's unhappiness, he laughed and said: 'No harm shall come to you, my friend. What quantity of kunafah do you require?'

'Five ounces,' muttered Ma'aruf.

'I will gladly let you have it,' said the cook, 'and you can pay me some other time.'

He cut a large slice of kunafah and added: 'I fear that I have no honey, but only sugar-cane syrup. I assure you it is just as good.'

The cook put the kunafah in a dish and poured syrup and melted butter over it until it was worthy of a king's table. Then he handed the dish to the cobbler, together with a cheese and a loaf of bread for his supper. Ma'aruf could scarcely find words to express his gratitude and, calling down fervent blessings on the good man, went off to his house.

As soon as his wife saw him she cried: 'Have you brought me the kunafah?'

Ma'aruf placed the dish before her, but no sooner had the vixen set eyes on the cake than she burst out in a menacing voice: 'Did I not tell you it must be made with honey? You have brought me a syrup cake to spite me! Did you think I would not know the difference?'

Abjectly Ma'aruf stammered out his explanation, saying: 'Good wife, I did not buy this cake; it was given me on credit by the kind-hearted pastry-cook.'

'This babble will not help you!' shrieked the furious woman. 'There, take your miserable syrup dish!' And she flung the cake in her husband's face and ordered him to go and fetch her another made with honey. Then she dealt him a savage blow on the jaw, knocking out one of his teeth, so that the blood trickled down his beard and chest.

Losing all patience, the long-suffering Ma'aruf impulsively lifted his hand and gave the woman a mild slap on the head. At this the termagant flew into a desperate rage; she gripped his beard with both her hands, and, raising her voice to its loudest pitch, shrieked out: 'Help, good Moslems! Help, my husband is murdering me!'

Hearing her cries, the neighbours came rushing into the house. After a long struggle they succeeded in freeing the cobbler's beard from his wife's clutches, but when they saw the injury she had inflicted on him and heard the cause of the dispute, they rebuked her and said: 'We are all content to eat syrup kunafah, and find it as good as the other kind. What has your poor husband done that you should torment him so?'

At length, thinking that peace had been restored between husband and wife, the neighbours went their way. Left alone with Fatimah, Ma'aruf attempted to pacify her. He gathered up the scattered remnants of the kunafah and offered it to her with a trembling hand, saying: 'Eat a little of this, my love, and tomorrow, if Allah wills, I shall bring you a kunafah dripping with honey.'

But the shrew gave no heed to his entreaties and swore that nothing would persuade her to touch it. At last, beginning to feel the pangs of hunger, Ma'aruf sat down to eat the kunafah himself. This he did to the accompaniment of an uninterrupted flow of abuse from his wife; and she continued to call down curses on him throughout the night.

Early next morning Ma'aruf went to the mosque and prayed to Allah to grant him the means wherewith to gratify his wife's demand. Then he opened his shop, but had scarcely sat down to his work when two guards burst in upon him, saying: 'We hold a warrant from the Cadi So-and-so for your arrest.' With this they manacled the cobbler and dragged him to their master's court.

When he was led into the Cadi's presence, Ma'aruf saw his wife standing all in tears, with a bandaged arm and her head wrapped in a blood-stained veil.

'Wretch!' cried the Cadi, as soon as he set eyes on Ma'aruf. 'Have you no fear of Allah that you beat this poor woman and break her arm and knock out her tooth?'

The cobbler was utterly confounded, and proceeded to tell the Cadi what had passed between him and his wife. Convinced that the unhappy man was telling the truth, the Cadi took pity on Ma'aruf and gave him a quarter of a dinar, saying: 'Take this and buy her a honey kunafah.' Then he exhorted the pair to use each other kindly and, having made peace between them, dismissed them from his presence.

Ma'aruf gave his wife the quarter of a dinar and returned to his shop. Presently, however, the guards who had marched him to the court came back to demand payment. When Ma'aruf told them that he had not a copper in his purse, they dragged him out into the market-place and would have given him a sound beating had he not instantly sold his cobbler's tools and paid them half a dinar.

As he sat in his empty shop brooding over his ill fortune, two ruffianly guards from the court of another cadi burst in, saying: 'We have a warrant for your arrest.' Without more ado they led him to the court, where Ma'aruf was astounded to see his wife standing as before, with bandaged arm and a blood-stained veil about her head, heaping up monstrous charges against him.

Again the cobbler related his story to the judge, adding: 'The Cadi So-and-so had but an hour ago made peace between us.'

'Woman,' cried the Cadi, addressing the shrew, 'if you are already reconciled, why have you come to me?'

'He has beaten me again!' protested Fatimah.

The Cadi rebuked them both and, after ordering Ma'aruf to pay the guards, dismissed them from his presence.

The harassed cobbler parted with his last copper and trudged dolefully back to his shop. Scarcely an hour had passed, when one of his friends came running to the door and cried: 'Rise, Ma'aruf, and fly for your life, for the shrew has brought an action against you at the Governor's court! His guards are even now on their way to arrest you!'

The terrified cobbler closed his shop and made off towards the Victory Gate. It was a grey winter afternoon, and as soon as he came to the outskirts of the city and found himself amongst the garbage heaps the rain began to fall in torrents, drenching him to the skin. On and on he ran, and at nightfall came to a ruined hovel where he took shelter from the storm. He sat down on the ground and wept bitterly, crying: 'Oh, how shall I save myself from this fiend? O Allah, help me fly to some far-off land, where I shall never see her more!'

Whilst he was thus lamenting, the wall of the hovel suddenly opened and there appeared before him a colossal jinnee whose fearsome aspect struck terror in his soul.

'Son of Adam,' roared the jinnee, 'what calamity can have befallen you that you disturb my midnight slumbers with your wailing? I am the jinnee of this ruin and have dwelt here these hundred years; yet have I never seen the like of this behaviour.' Then, moved with pity, the jinnee added: 'Tell me what you desire, and I will do your bidding.'

Ma'aruf told him the story of his misfortunes, and the jinnee said: 'Mount on my back, and I will take you to a land where your wife shall never find you.'

The cobbler climbed onto the back of the jinnee, who flew with him between earth and sky all night and at daybreak set him down on the top of a mountain.

'Son of Adam,' said the jinnee, 'go down this mountain and you will come to the gates of Ikhtiyan-al-Khatan. In that city you will find refuge from your wife.' And, so saying, the jinnee vanished.

Amazed and bewildered, Ma'aruf remained where the jinnee had left him until the sun rose. Then he climbed down the mountain and at length came to a well-built city surrounded by high walls. He entered the gates, and, as he walked through the streets, the townsfolk stared at him with wondering eyes and gathered about him, marvelling at his strange costume. Presently a man stepped forward and asked him whence he had come.

'From Cairo,' replied Ma'aruf.

'When did you leave Cairo?' inquired the man.

'Last night,' he answered, 'just after the hour of evening prayers.'

At these words his questioner laughed incredulously, and, turning to the bystanders, cried: 'Listen to this mad-man! He tells us that he left Cairo only last night!'

The crowd greeted this remark with loud laughter, and, pressing round Ma'aruf, shouted: 'Have you taken leave of your senses? How was it that you left Cairo only last night? Do you not know that Cairo is a year's journey from this city?'

Ma'aruf swore that he was speaking the truth, and to prove his story took from his pocket a loaf of Cairo bread and showed it to them. They were all astonished to see the loaf, which was of a kind unknown in their country, and still soft and fresh. A few believed him, whilst others ridiculed him. As this was going forward, a wealthy merchant, followed by two slaves, came riding by and, stopping near the crowd, admonished them sternly, saying: 'Are you not ashamed to make game of this stranger?'

Then, turning to Ma'aruf, the merchant spoke to him kindly and invited him to his house.

There his host clad Ma'aruf in a merchant's robe worth a thousand dinars, seated him in a splendid hall, and entertained him at a sumptuous meal. When they had finished eating, the merchant said to the cobbler: 'Pray tell me, my brother, what land you have come from, for by your dress you would seem to be an Egyptian.'

'You are right, my master,' replied Ma'aruf. 'I am an Egyptian, and Cairo is the city of my birth.'

'What is your trade?' inquired the merchant.

'I am a cobbler; I patch old shoes.'

'In what part of Cairo did you live?'

'In Red Lane,' replied Ma'aruf.

'What folk do you know there?'

Ma'aruf named several of his neighbours in that street.

'Do you know Sheikh Ahmed the perfume-seller?' asked the merchant eagerly.

'Do I know him?' laughed Ma'aruf. 'Why, he is my nextdoor neighbour!'

'How is he faring?'

'Thanks be to Allah, he is in the best of health,' replied the cobbler.

'How many sons has he now?'

'He has three sons: Mustapha, Mohammed, and Ali.'

'What do they do for their living?' inquired the host.

'The eldest, Mustapha,' replied Ma'aruf, 'is a school-master. Mohammed, the second, is a perfume-seller and has set up a shop of his own next to his father's. His wife has but recently borne him a son, whom they called Hassan. As for Ali, he was the playmate of my childhood. Together we would enter the churches of the Christians and steal their prayer books; then we would sell them in the market-place and buy sweet-meats with the money. One day the Christians caught us red-handed and complained to our parents. They threatened Ali's father, saying: "If you do not restrain your son, we will inform the King of this sacrilege." Sheikh Ahmed gave his son a thrashing and poor little Ali ran away from home. No news has been heard of him these twenty years.'

Here the merchant threw his arms round the cobbler's neck and wept for joy, crying: 'Praise be to Allah! O Ma'aruf, I am that very Ali, the son of Sheikh Ahmed the perfume-seller!'

Then Ali asked his friend what had brought him to Ikhtiyan-al-Khatan, and the cobbler recounted to him the tale of his misfortunes and all that had befallen him since his disastrous marriage. He explained how he had chosen to flee the city rather than remain at the mercy of his heartless wife, how he met the jinnee in the ruined hovel, and how he was carried overnight to Ikhtiyan-al-Khatan. Then Ma'aruf asked his friend to tell him how he rose to such prosperity.

'After I left Cairo,' said Ali, 'I wandered for many years from place to place and at length arrived, forlorn and penniless, in this city. I found its people honest and kind-hearted, hospitable to strangers and always ready to help the poor. I told them that I was a rich merchant, the owner of a great caravan which would shortly arrive in their city. They believed my story and gave me a splendid mansion for my use. Then I borrowed a thousand dinars, telling my creditor that I needed a few necessities before my merchandise arrived. With this money I bought a quantity of goods and sold them the following day at a profit of fifty pieces of gold. I bought more goods, and, to enhance my reputation, I sought the acquaintance of the richest merchants in the town and entertained them liberally in my house. I continued to buy and sell until I had amassed a large fortune.

'The old proverb says: "Where candour fails, cunning thrives." Now, my friend, if you tell the people of this city that you are a poor cobbler, that you have run away from a nagging wife and left Cairo only yesterday, no one will believe you and you will become the laughing stock of the whole town. If you tell them that you were carried here by a jinnee, you will frighten everyone away and they will think: "This man is possessed with an evil spirit." No, my friend, this will not do.'

'Then what am I to do?' asked the perplexed Ma'aruf.

'Tomorrow morning,' said Ali, 'you shall mount my finest mule and ride to the market-place, with one of my slaves walking behind you all the way. There you will find me sitting among the richest merchants of the city. When I see you I will rise and greet you, I will kiss your hand and receive you with the utmost deference. When you have taken your seat among the other merchants, I shall question you about many kinds of merchandise, saying: "Have you such-and-such a cloth?" And you must answer: "Plenty! Plenty!" When they ask me who you are, I shall say you are a merchant of great wealth, and praise your munificence. If a beggar holds out his hand to you, give him gold. These proceedings will earn you great consideration in the merchants' eyes. They will seek your acquaintance and wish to trade with you, and before long you will become indeed a merchant of great wealth.'

Next morning Ali dressed Ma'aruf in a magnificent robe, gave him a thousand dinars, and mounted him upon his best mule. At the appointed time the cobbler rode to the market-place, where he found his friend sitting among the merchants. As soon as Ali saw him approaching he rose, threw himself at his feet, kissed his hand, and helped him from his mule, saying: 'May your day be blessed, great Ma'aruf!'

When the newcomer had gravely taken his seat, the wondering merchants came to Ali one after another and asked him in a low voice: 'Who may this sheikh be?' Ali replied: 'He is one of the chief merchants of Egypt. His wealth and the wealth of his father and forefathers is of proverbial fame, and his munificence is boundless as the sea. He possesses shops and storehouses in all the corners of the earth, and his agents and partners are the pillars of commerce in every city from Egypt and Yemen to India and the far-flung hills of Sind. Indeed the wealthiest merchant in this city is but a poor pedlar when compared with him.'

Hearing this encomium, the merchants thronged around Ma'aruf, vying with each other to welcome him and offering him sherbets. The chief of the merchants himself came to greet him, and questioned him eagerly about the goods he had brought.

'Doubtless, my master,' he said, 'you have many bales of yellow silk?'

'Plenty! Plenty!' answered Ma'aruf, without a moment's hesitation.

'And gazelle blood-red?' asked another.

'Plenty! Plenty!' replied the cobbler gravely.

To all their questions he made the same answer, and when one of the merchants begged him to show them a few samples, Ma'aruf replied: 'Certainly, as soon as my caravan arrives.' Then he explained to the company that he was expecting a caravan of a thousand mules within the next few days.

Now whilst the merchants were chatting together and marvelling at the extraordinary richness of the caravan, a beggar came round and held out his hand to each in turn. A few gave him half a dirham, some a copper, but most of them gave him nothing. Ma'aruf, however, calmly drew out a handful of gold and gave it to the beggar.

The merchants marvelled at this, and thought to themselves: 'By Allah, this man must be richer than a king!'

Then a poor woman approached him, and to her also he gave a handful of gold. Scarcely believing her eyes, the woman hurried away to tell the other beggars and they all came flocking round Ma'aruf with outstretched hands. The cobbler gave each a handful of gold, until the thousand dinars were finished. Then he clapped his hands together, saying: 'By Allah, to think there are so many beggars in this city! Had I known of this I would have come prepared, for it is not my way to refuse alms. What shall I do now if a beggar solicits me before my caravan arrives? If only I had, say, a thousand dinars!'

'Do not let that trouble you,' said the chief of the merchants. And he at once sent for a thousand dinars and handed the money to Ma'aruf.

The cobbler continued to give gold to every beggar who passed by. When the muezzin's call summoned the Faithful to afternoon prayers, he went with the merchants to the mosque, and what remained of the thousand dinars he scattered over the heads of the worshippers.

As soon as the prayers were over he borrowed another thousand, and these also he gave away. By nightfall Ma'aruf had obtained five thousand dinars from the merchants and given them all away, while the dismayed Ali watched the proceedings helplessly. And to all his creditors he said: 'When my caravan arrives, if you want gold, you shall have gold; and if you want goods, you shall have goods: for I have vast quantities of them.'

That night Ali entertained the merchants at his house. Ma'aruf was given the seat of honour, and all night spoke of nothing but jewels and rich silks. And whenever they asked him if he had this or that merchandise in his caravan, the cobbler replied: 'Plenty! Plenty!'

Next morning he again went to the market-place, where he talked to the merchants about his caravan and borrowed more money and gave it to the beggars. This he repeated each day for twenty days, and by the end of this time he had taken sixty thousand pieces of gold on credit. And still no caravan arrived: no, not as much as a half-cooked pie.

At length the merchants, who were becoming impatient at the caravan's delay, began to clamour for their money. They voiced their anxiety to their friend Ali, who, himself alarmed at the cobbler's munificence, took him aside and remonstrated with him, saying: 'Have you taken leave of your senses? I told you to toast the bread, not to burn it! The merchants are demanding their money and say that you owe them sixty thousand dinars. You have squandered all this gold among the beggars: how will you ever pay it back, idle as you are, with no work to do or goods to trade with?'

'No matter,' replied Ma'aruf. 'What is sixty thousand dinars? When my caravan arrives, if they want gold, they shall have gold; and if they want goods, they shall have goods: for I have vast quantities of them.'

'Now glory be to Allah!' exclaimed Ali. 'What goods are you talking about?'

'Why, the goods in my caravan,' replied Ma'aruf. 'I have countless bales of merchandise.'

'Impudent dog!' cried Ali. 'Are you telling me that story? Why, I will denounce you to the whole world!'

'Be off!' said Ma'aruf. 'Did you suppose I was a poor man? Know, then, I have priceless riches on the way. As soon as my caravan arrives, the merchants shall be repaid twofold!'

At this Ali grew very angry and cried: 'Scoundrel! I will teach you to lie to me!'

'Do your worst!' replied the cobbler. 'They must wait until my caravan arrives, and then they shall have their money back and more.'

In despair Ali left Ma'aruf and went away thinking: 'If

I now abuse him after so highly commending him, I shall, as the saying goes, be a twofold liar.'

When the merchants returned, inquiring the outcome of his audience with Ma'aruf, the harassed Ali replied: 'My friends, I had not the heart to speak to him about his debts, for I myself have lent him a thousand dinars. When you advanced him so much money, you did not seek my advice; therefore you cannot hold me responsible. Speak to him yourselves. If he fails to pay his debts, denounce him to the King as an impostor and a thief.'

The merchants went in a body to the King and told him all that had passed between them and Ma'aruf. 'Your majesty,' they said, 'we are in great perplexity about this merchant, whose generosity knows no bounds. He has borrowed sixty thousand dinars from us and scattered them in handfuls among the poor. Were he a poor man, he would never be so foolish as to squander such a fortune; and if he is indeed a man of wealth, why has his vaunted caravan not yet arrived?'

Now the King was an avaricious old miser. When he heard the merchants' account of Ma'aruf's prodigality, greed took possession of his soul and he said to his Vizier: 'This merchant must surely be a man of extraordinary wealth, or he would never have been capable of such munificence. His caravan is certain to arrive. Now I will not suffer these wolves of the market-place to grab all the treasures for themselves, for they are already too rich. I must seek his friendship, so that when his caravan arrives I, too, will have a share. Why, I might even give him my daughter in marriage and join his wealth to mine.'

But the Vizier replied: 'This man is an impostor, your majesty. Beware of avarice, for avarice brings ruin and repentance.'

'I will put him to the test,' said the King, 'and we will soon discover if he is a trickster. I will show him a costly pearl and ask him his opinion. If he can tell its worth, we shall know that he is a man of affluence accustomed to such rarities. If he cannot, then we shall know that he is a liar and a fraud, and I will put him to a cruel death.'

The Vizier sent at once for Ma'aruf, and when he had been admitted to the King's presence and exchanged greetings with him, the King asked: 'Is it true that you owe the merchants sixty thousand pieces of gold?'

When Ma'aruf replied that it was true, he asked: 'Why do you not pay them their money?'

'The day my caravan arrives,' replied Ma'aruf, 'they shall be paid twofold. If they want gold, they shall have gold; if they want silver, they shall have silver; and if they prefer goods, they shall have goods: for I have vast quantities of them.'

Then, to test Ma'aruf, the King handed him a rare pearl worth a thousand dinars. 'Have you such pearls in your caravan?' he asked.

Ma'aruf examined the pearl for a moment, and, throwing it disdainfully to the ground, crushed it beneath his heel.

'What is the meaning of this?' cried the King indignantly.

'This pearl,' replied the cobbler with a laugh, 'is scarcely worth a thousand dinars. I have vast quantities of infinitely larger pearls in my caravan.'

At this the King's avarice knew no bounds. He at once sent for the merchants, told them that their fears were groundless, and assured them that the caravan would soon arrive. Then he summoned the Vizier and said: 'See that the merchant Ma'aruf is received with all magnificence at the palace. Speak to him about my daughter the Princess. Perhaps he will consent to marry her and so we shall gain possession of all his wealth.'

'Your majesty,' replied the Vizier, 'I do not like the manner of this foreigner. His presence bodes evil to the court. I pray you to wait until we have visible proof of his caravan.'

Now the Vizier himself had once sought the Princess's hand in marriage and his suit had been rejected. So when the King heard this warning, he flew into a passion and cried: 'Treacherous dog, you slander this merchant only because you wish to marry the Princess yourself. You would have her left on my hands until she is old and unacceptable. Could she ever find a more suitable husband than this accomplished, generous, and opulent young man? Not only will he make her a perfect husband, but he will make us all rich into the bargain!'

Afraid of the King's anger, the Vizier kept his own counsel and said no more. He betook himself to Ma'aruf and said to him: 'His majesty the King desires you to marry his daughter the Princess. What answer shall I give him?'

'I am honoured by the King's proposal,' replied Ma'aruf with an air of dignified reserve. 'But do you not think it would be better to wait until my caravan arrives? The dowry of such a bride as the Princess would be a greater expense than I can at present afford. I must give my wife a marriage-portion of at least five thousand purses of gold. Among the poor of the city I shall have to distribute a thousand purses on the bridal night; to those who walk in the wedding procession I must give a thousand more; and I shall need another thousand to entertain the troops. On the next morning I must present a hundred rich diamonds to the Princess, and as many jewels to the slave-girls and the eunuchs of the palace. All this is an expense which cannot be met before my caravan arrives.'

When the Vizier went back to the King and repeated to him Ma'aruf's reply, the King was overwhelmed at the prodigious recital and sent the Vizier to bring him to his presence. As soon as the cobbler entered the King said: 'Honoured and most distinguished merchant, let us celebrate this happy union forthwith! I myself will meet the expenses of the marriage. My treasury is full; I give you leave to take from it all that you require. You can settle the Princess's dowry when your caravan comes in. By Allah, I will take no refusal!'

Without a moment's delay the King sent for the Imam of the royal mosque, who drew up a marriage contract for Ma'aruf and the Princess.

The city was gaily decorated at the King's orders, drums and trumpets sounded in the streets, and Ma'aruf the cobbler sat enthroned in the great parlour of the palace. A troupe of singers, dancers, wrestlers, clowns, and acrobats capered round the court to entertain the guests, whilst the royal treasurer brought Ma'aruf bag after bag of gold to scatter among the merry throng. He had no rest that day, for no sooner had he come to Ma'aruf staggering under the weight of a hundred thousand dinars, than he was sent back for another load. The Vizier watched the spectacle with rage in his heart, whilst Ali the merchant, aghast at the proceedings, approached Ma'aruf and whispered in his ear: 'May Allah have no mercy upon you! Is it not enough that you have frittered away the wealth of all the merchants? Must you also drain the royal treasury?'

'What is that to you?' replied Ma'aruf. 'Be sure that when my great caravan arrives, I will repay the King a thousandfold.'

The extravagant rejoicings lasted forty days, and then came the wedding day. The King, accompanied by his viziers and the officers of his troops, walked in the bridal procession, and as he passed by, Ma'aruf threw handfuls of gold to the crowds that lined their way.

When the couple were at length left alone in the bridal chamber, and the Princess lay down beneath the velvet curtains of the bed, Ma'aruf sat on the floor and wrung his hands in despair. Perceiving his grief, the princess tenderly asked him: 'Why so sad, my lord?'

'There is no strength or help save in Allah!' replied Ma'aruf with a sigh. 'It is all your father's fault!'

'How so?' she asked.

'He has exposed me to ridicule in the eyes of the whole world!' sighed Ma'aruf. 'Surely everyone must have noticed my meanness, my miserly treatment of you and the royal guests! If only he had waited till my great caravan arrived! At least I should have been able to give you a few rich presents befitting your degree, and bestow upon your women jewels and ornaments in honour of this happy occasion. But your father would hurry on the wedding and put me to this shame! It was like burning green grass!'

'Instead of worrying about such trifles,' replied the Princess, 'undress and come to bed. Put away all thoughts of presents and caravans, my dear, and gird your loins for the merry sport!'

Ma'aruf cast off his clothes and, climbing into bed, threw himself upon the Princess as she lay on her back. He clasped her tight, and she pressed close to him, so that tongue met tongue in that hour when men forget their mothers. He slipped his hands under her armpits and strained her to his breast, squeezing all the honey and setting the dainties face to face. Then, threading the needle, he kindled the match, put it to the priming, and fired the shot. Thus the citadel was breached and the victory won.

After a night of such dalliance, Ma'aruf rose and went to the bath. Then he dressed himself in a princely robe and entered the King's council-chamber, where he sat down by the side of his father-in-law to receive the felicitations of the viziers and the chief officers of the kingdom. He sent for the treasurer and ordered him to give robes of honour to all who were present; then he called for sacks of gold and gave handfuls to every member of the royal palace from the highest courtier to the humblest kitchen boy. And for twenty days he thus continued to dissipate the King's treasure.

At the end of this time there was still no news of Ma'aruf's caravan, and at length the day came when the

treasurer found his coffers empty. He went to the King
with a heavy heart and said: 'Your majesty, the treasure
chests are empty and the great caravan of your son-in-law
has not yet come to fill them.'

Alarmed at these words, the King turned to his Vizier
and said: 'By Allah, it is true there is still no sign of the
caravan. What shall we do?'

'Allah prolong your days, my master,' replied the
Vizier with an evil smile. 'Did I not warn you against
the wiles of this impostor? I swear he has no caravan:
no, not as much as a half-cooked pie! He has married
your daughter without a dowry and defrauded you of
all your treasure. How long will your majesty tolerate
this vagabond?'

'If only we could find the truth about him!' sighed the
King in great perplexity.

'Your majesty,' said the Vizier, 'no one is better able
to find out a man's secrets than his wife. I beg you to
call your daughter here and permit me to question her
from behind the curtain.'

'It shall be done!' replied the King. 'On my life, if it be
proved that he has deceived us, he shall die the cruellest
of deaths!'

At once the King had a curtain drawn across the hall,
and, summoning the Princess, bade her sit behind it and
speak with the Vizier.

'What do you wish to know?' she asked.

'Honoured lady,' began the Vizier, 'the chests of the
treasury are empty, thanks to the extravagance of the
Prince Ma'aruf, and the wondrous caravan, about which
we have heard so much, has not yet come. Therefore

the King has given me leave to ask what you know of this stranger and whether you have reason to suspect him.'

'Night after night,' replied the Princess, 'he has promised me pearls and jewels, and treasures without number. But of these I have yet seen nothing.'

'Your highness,' said the Vizier, 'I counsel you to question him tonight, that we may know the answer to this riddle. Beg him to tell you the truth, and promise to keep his secret.'

'I hear and obey,' replied the Princess. 'I will speak to Ma'aruf tonight and tell you what he says.'

In the evening, when the pair lay side by side, the Princess threw her arms around Ma'aruf and, assuming that sweet and endearing air with which subtle women coax their husbands, said to him: 'Light of my eyes and flower of my heart, may Time and Destiny never part us! Your love has kindled in my breast such fires that I will gladly die for you. Tell me the truth about your caravan and conceal nothing from me. How long will you delude my father with such lies? For I fear that he will find you out at last and make you pay dearly for this deception. Tell me everything, my love, and I will contrive a means to help you.'

'Sweet Princess,' replied Ma'aruf, 'I will tell you all. I am no wealthy merchant, no master of caravans. In my own land I was a poor cobbler, cursed with a vixen of a wife called . . .' And he recounted to the Princess the tale of his connubial misfortunes from the adventure of the honey-cake to his flight to Ikhtiyan-al-Khatan.

When she heard the cobbler's story, the Princess burst

into a fit of laughter and said: 'Truly, Ma'aruf, you are a subtle rogue! But what are we to do? What will my father say when he learns the truth? The Vizier has already sown suspicions in his mind. He will surely kill you, and I shall die of grief. Take this fifty thousand dinars and leave the palace this very hour. Ride away to some far country, and then send a courier to acquaint me with your news.'

'I am at your mercy, mistress,' replied the cobbler.

After he had dallied with the Princess for a while, he rose, disguised himself in the livery of a slave and, mounting the fastest horse in the King's stables, rode out into the night.

Next morning, the King sat in the council-chamber with the Vizier by his side and summoned the Princess to his presence. When she had taken her seat behind the curtain as before, the King asked: 'Tell us, my daughter, what you have learned about Prince Ma'aruf.'

'May Allah confound all slanderous tongues,' exclaimed the Princess, 'and blacken the face of your Vizier, as he would have blackened mine in my husband's eyes!'

'How so?' asked the King.

'Last night,' continued the Princess, 'soon after my husband came to my chamber, the chief of the eunuchs brought in a letter from ten richly dressed slaves who begged an audience with their master Ma'aruf. I took the letter and read aloud: "From the five hundred slaves of the caravan to their master the merchant Ma'aruf. We would have you know that soon after you left us we were attacked by a host of two thousand mounted bedouin. A bloody battle ensued, and lasted thirty days and thirty nights. The caravan lost fifty of its slaves, a hundred mules, and two hundred loads of merchandise. This is the cause of our delay."

'Yet at this bad news the Prince was undismayed; he did not even ask further details from the waiting messengers. "What are two hundred bales and a hundred wretched mules?" he said. "At worst the loss cannot be more than seventy thousand pieces of gold. Think no more about it, my dear. One thing alone distresses me, that I shall have to leave you for a few days in order to go myself and hasten the arrival of the caravan." He rose with a carefree laugh, embraced me tenderly, and bade me farewell. When he had gone I looked through the window of my chamber and saw him chatting with ten handsome slaves dressed in uniforms of rare magnificence. Presently he mounted his horse and rode away with them to bring the caravan home. Allah be praised that I did not question my husband in the manner you requested,' added the Princess bitterly. 'I would have lost his love and he would have ceased to trust me. It was all the fault of your hateful Vizier, whose only thought is to revile my husband and discredit him in your eyes.'

The King rejoiced at these words and exclaimed: 'May Allah increase your husband's wealth and prolong his years, my daughter!' Then, turning to the Vizier, he rebuked him angrily and bade him henceforth hold his tongue. So much for the King, the Vizier, and the Princess.

As for Ma'aruf, he journeyed disconsolately far into the desert, his heart yearning for his beloved princess, until he came at midday to the outskirts of a little village.

By this time he was tired and very hungry. Seeing a ploughman driving two oxen in a field, he went up to him and greeted him, saying: 'Peace be with you!'

The peasant returned his greeting and, noticing the stranger's garb, inquired: 'Doubtless, my master, you are one of the King's servants?'

When Ma'aruf replied that he was, the ploughman welcomed him, saying: 'Pray dismount and be my guest this day!'

The cobbler thanked the poor peasant for his generosity and politely declined. But the kind old man would take no refusal. 'Pray dismount,' he insisted, 'and grant me the honour of entertaining you. I will go instantly to the village, which is close at hand, and bring you food and hay for your horse.'

'Since the village is so near, my friend,' protested Ma'aruf, 'I can easily ride there myself and buy food in the market-place.'

But the peasant smiled and shook his head. 'I fear you will find no market-place in a poor hamlet such as ours,' he replied. 'I beg you, in Allah's name, to rest here with your horse while I quickly run to the village.'

Not wishing to offend the old man, Ma'aruf dismounted and sat down on the grass, while his host hurried away.

As he waited for the peasant's return, Ma'aruf thought: 'I am keeping this poor man from his work. I will make up for his lost time by working at the plough myself.'

He rose and, going up to the oxen, drove the plough along the furrow. The beasts had not gone far, however, when the share struck against an object in the ground and came to a sudden halt. Ma'aruf goaded the oxen on but, though they strained powerfully against the yoke, the plough remained rooted in the ground. Clearing away the soil about the share, Ma'aruf found that it had caught in a great ring of gold set in a marble slab the size of a large millstone. He exerted all his strength, and when he had moved the slab aside, he saw below it a flight of stairs. Going down the stairs he found himself in a square vault as large as the city baths containing four separate halls. The first was filled with gold from floor to ceiling; the second with pearls, emeralds, and coral; the third with jacinths, rubies, and turquoises; and the fourth with diamonds and other precious stones. At the far side of the vault stood a coffer of clearest crystal and upon it a golden casket no larger than a lemon.

The cobbler marvelled and rejoiced at this discovery. He went up to the little casket and, lifting its lid, found in it a gold signet ring finely engraved with strange talismanic inscriptions that resembled the legs of creeping insects. He slipped the ring upon his finger and, as he did so, rubbed the seal.

At once a mighty jinnee appeared before him, saying: 'I am here, master, I am here! Speak and I will obey! What is your wish? Would you have me build a capital, or lay a town in ruin? Would you have me slay a king, or dig a river-bed? I am your slave, by order of the Sovereign of the Jinn, Creator of the day and night! What is your wish?'

Amazed at the apparition, Ma'aruf cried: 'Creature of Allah, who are you?'

'I am Abul-Sa'adah, the slave of the ring,' replied the

jinnee. 'Faithfully I serve my master, and my master is he who rubs the ring. Nothing is beyond my power; for I am lord over seventy-two tribes of jinn, each two-and-seventy thousand strong: each jinnee rules over a thousand giants, each giant over a thousand goblins, each goblin over a thousand demons, and each demon over a thousand imps. All these owe me absolute allegiance; and yet for all my power, I cannot choose but to obey my master. Ask what you will, and it shall be done. Be it on land or sea, by day or night: should you need me you have but to rub the ring, and I will be at hand to do your bidding. Of one thing only I must warn you; if you rub the ring twice I shall be consumed in the fire of the powerful words engraved on the seal, and you will lose me for ever.'

'Abul-Sa'adah,' said Ma'aruf, 'can you tell me what this place is, and who imprisoned you in this ring?'

'This vault in which you stand, my master,' replied the jinnee, 'is the ancient treasure-house of Shaddad Ibn Aad, King of the many-columned city of Iram. While he lived I was his servant and dwelt in this ring. Just before his death he locked it away in this treasure-house, and it was your good fortune to find it.'

'Slave of the ring,' said the cobbler, 'can you carry all this treasure to the open?'

'That is very easy,' replied the jinnee.

'Then do so without delay,' said Ma'aruf, 'and leave nothing in this vault.'

Scarcely had he uttered these words when the earth opened and there appeared before him several handsome youths with baskets upon their heads. These they quickly filled with gold and jewels and carried them above ground; and in a few moments the four halls were emptied of their treasure.

'Who are these boys?' asked Ma'aruf.

'They are my own sons,' replied the jinnee. 'A light task such as this does not require the mustering of a mighty band of jinn. What else do you wish, my master?'

'I require a train of mules loaded with chests,' replied Ma'aruf, 'to carry these marvels to Ikhtiyan-al-Khatan.'

The jinnee uttered a great cry, and there appeared seven hundred richly saddled mules laden with chests and baskets, and a hundred slaves magnificently clad. In a twinkling the chests and baskets were filled with treasure and placed upon the mules, and the caravan stood in splendid array, guarded by mounted slaves.

'And now, slave of the ring,' said Ma'aruf, 'I require a few hundred loads of precious stuffs.'

'Would you have Syrian damask or Persian velvet, Indian brocade or Roman silk or Egyptian gaberdine?'

'A hundred loads of each!' cried Ma'aruf.

'I hear and obey,' replied the slave. 'I will at once dispatch my jinn to those distant lands, and they shall return tomorrow morning with all that you require.'

Then Ma'aruf ordered the slave of the ring to set up a pavilion and serve him food and wine. The jinnee promptly provided his master with a silk pavilion and a sumptuous meal, and departed on his mission.

As Ma'aruf was about to sit down to his feast, the old peasant returned from the village, carrying a large bowl of lentils for his guest and a sack of hay for the horse. When he saw the great caravan drawn up in the field, and

Ma'aruf reclining in the tent, attended by innumerable slaves, he thought that his guest must be no other than the King. 'I will hurry back,' he reflected, 'and kill my two fowls and roast them in butter for him.'

The peasant was on the point of turning back when Ma'aruf saw him and ordered his slaves to bring him into the pavilion.

The slaves led the peasant to the tent, with his bowl of lentils and his sack of hay. Ma'aruf rose to receive him and welcomed him, saying: 'What is it you are carrying, my brother?'

'My master,' replied the peasant, all abashed, 'I was bringing you your dinner and some hay for your horse. Forgive my scant courtesy, I pray you. Had I known you were the King, I would have killed my two fowls and roasted them in butter for you.'

'Do not be dismayed, my friend,' replied Ma'aruf, 'I am not the King, but only his son-in-law. A certain misunderstanding arose between us and I left the palace. He has sent these messengers to fetch me and these presents as a token of his forgiveness. Tomorrow morning I shall return to the city.' Then Ma'aruf thanked the peasant for his generosity and seated him by his side, saying: 'By Allah, I will eat nothing but the food of your hospitality.'

He ordered the slaves to serve the peasant with the choice meats and ate the lentils himself. When the meal was finished he filled the empty bowl with gold and gave it to the peasant. 'Take this to your family,' he said, 'and if you come to see me at the palace, you shall receive a hearty welcome and a generous reward.'

The peasant took the gold and returned to the village, scarcely believing his good fortune.

When darkness fell, the slaves of the caravan brought into the tent beautiful young girls, who danced and made music. At daybreak Ma'aruf perceived a great cloud of dust in the distance and presently saw a long procession of mules approaching. They were laden with innumerable bales of merchandise, and at their head rode the jinnee in the semblance of a caravan-leader, alongside a four-pillared litter of pure gold inlaid with diamonds. When the caravan came to the tent, the jinnee dismounted and, kissing the ground before Ma'aruf, said: 'The task is accomplished, my master. Pray mount into this litter and put on the garment which I have brought especially for you. You will find it worthy of a king.'

'One thing more remains to be done,' said Ma'aruf. 'Before I set forth with the caravan, I wish you to hasten to Ikhtiyan-al-Khatan and announce my coming to the King.'

'I hear and obey,' replied the jinnee, and instantly transforming himself into the semblance of a courier made off towards the city.

He arrived at the palace just as the Vizier was saying to the King: 'Be no longer deceived, your majesty, by the lies of this impostor. Give no credence to your daughter's story; for I swear by your precious life that it was not to hurry on the arrival of his caravan that Prince Ma'aruf fled the city, but to save his skin.'

The Vizier had not finished speaking, when the courier entered the royal presence and kissed the ground before the King, saying: 'Your majesty, I bring you greetings from the illustrious Prince your son-in-law, who is now approaching the city with his noble caravan.'

With this the courier again kissed the ground before the King and hurried out of the palace. The King rejoiced, and, turning to the Vizier, exclaimed: 'May Allah blacken your face, traitor of ill omen! How long will you revile my son-in-law to my face and call him a thief and a liar?'

The dumbfounded Vizier hung his head, whilst the King hastened to give orders for the decoration of the city and to send out a procession to meet the caravan. Then he went to his daughter's chamber and told her the joyful news. The Princess was astounded to hear her father speak of the caravan, and thought: 'Can this be another of Ma'aruf's tricks? Or was he testing my love with an invented tale of poverty?'

But even more astonished than the Princess was her husband's friend, Ali the merchant. When he beheld the great commotion in the city and learnt the news of Ma'aruf's imminent arrival at the head of a splendid caravan, he thought: 'What new roguery is this? Can it be possible that this patcher of old slippers is really coming with a caravan? Or is it some fresh trick which he has contrived with the aid of the Princess? May Allah preserve my old friend from dishonour!'

Before long the procession, which had gone out to meet the caravan, returned to the city. Arrayed in a magnificent robe, Ma'aruf rode triumphantly by the King's side in the golden litter and, as the interminable caravan wound its way through the streets, the merchants flocked around their prodigal debtor and kissed the ground before him as he passed. Ali the merchant pushed his way through the throng, and whispered to Ma'aruf: 'How has this come about, sheikh of mad swindlers? And yet, by Allah, you deserve your good fortune!'

The procession halted at the royal palace, and Ma'aruf sat with the King in the great council-chamber. He ordered his slaves to fill the royal coffers with gold and jewels, and to unpack the bales of precious merchandise. He chose the finest stuffs and said to the attendants: 'Carry these silks to the Princess that she may distribute them among her women; and take to her this chest of jewels that she may share its contents among the slaves and eunuchs.'

Then he proceeded to deal out the treasures to the officers of the King's army, to the courtiers and their wives, to his creditors the merchants, and to the poor of the city, while the King writhed upon his throne in an agony of greed. As Ma'aruf threw handfuls of pearls and emeralds to right and left, the King would whisper to him: 'Enough, my son! There will be nothing left for us!' But Ma'aruf would answer: 'My caravan is inexhaustible.'

Soon the Vizier came and told the King that the treasury was full and could hold no more. And the King cried: 'Fill another hall!'

Then Ma'aruf hastened to his wife, who received him in a transport of joy and kissed his hand, saying: 'Was it to mock me or to test my love that you pretended to be a poor cobbler fleeing from a nagging wife? Whichever it was, I thank Allah I did not fail you.'

Ma'aruf embraced her and gave her a gown splendidly embroidered in gold, a necklace threaded with forty orphan pearls, and a pair of anklets fashioned by the art of mighty sorcerers. His wife cried out for joy as she saw these marvels, and said: 'I will keep them for festivals and state occasions only.'

'Not so, my love,' replied Ma'aruf, 'I will give you ornaments like these each day.'

Then he summoned the slave-girls of the harem and bestowed upon each of them an embroidered robe, adorned with ornaments of gold. Arrayed in this splendour, they were like the black-eyed houris of Paradise, whilst the Princess shone in their midst like the moon amongst the stars.

At nightfall the King said to the Vizier: 'What have you to say now? Does not the wealth of my son-in-law surpass all wonders?'

'Indeed, your majesty,' replied the Vizier, 'the Prince's prodigality is that of no ordinary merchant; for where can a merchant find such pearls and jewels as your son-in-law has thrown away? Kings and princes have not treasures like these. There must surely be some strange reason for his conduct. I suggest, my master, that you make Prince Ma'aruf drunk if you wish to discover the source of his riches. When he is overcome with wine, we will ply him with questions until he tells us all. Indeed, I already fear the consequences of this extraordinary munificence, for it is more than likely that he will in time win the troops with his favours and drive you from your kingdom.'

'You have spoken wisely, my Vizier,' said the King. 'Tomorrow we must find out the whole truth.'

Next morning, whilst the King was sitting in his

council-chamber, the grooms of the royal stables rushed in, begging leave to speak with him. 'Your majesty,' they cried, 'the entire caravan of Prince Ma'aruf is gone! All the slaves, the horses, and the mules disappeared during the night, and nowhere can we find a trace of them.'

Greatly troubled at this news, the King hastened to Ma'aruf's chamber and told him what had happened. But Ma'aruf laughed aloud.

'Pray calm yourself, your majesty,' he said. 'The loss of these trifles is nothing to me. For what is a caravan of mules?'

'By Allah,' thought the King in amazement, 'what manner of man is this, to whom wealth counts for nothing? There must surely be a reason for all this!'

When evening came, the King sat with Ma'aruf and the Vizier in a pavilion in the garden of the palace. Wine flowed freely; and, when Ma'aruf was flushed with drink so that he could not tell his left hand from his right, the Vizier said to him: 'Your highness, you have never told us the adventures of your life. Pray let us hear how you achieved your prodigious wealth, and the marvellous vicissitudes of fortune which have befallen you.'

Thereupon the drunken cobbler related the story of his life, from his marriage in Cairo to the finding of the magic ring in the peasant's field.

Then said the Vizier: 'Will you not permit us to see the ring, your highness?'

Without a moment's thought the foolish cobbler slipped the ring from his finger and handed it to the Vizier, saying: 'Look at the seal! My servant the jinnee dwells within it!'

The Vizier instantly passed the ring upon his own finger and rubbed the seal; and the jinnee appeared before him, saying: 'I am here! Ask and receive! Would you have me build a capital, or lay a town in ruin? Would you have me slay a king, or dig a river-bed?'

'Slave of the ring,' replied the Vizier, pointing to Ma'aruf, 'take up this rascal and cast him down upon some barren desert where he shall perish from hunger and thirst!'

At once the jinnee snatched up Ma'aruf and flew with him between earth and sky until he set him down in the middle of a waterless desert.

Then said the Vizier to the King: 'Did I not tell you that this dog was a liar and a cheat? But you gave no heed to my counsel.'

'You were right, my Vizier,' replied the King. 'Give me the ring that I may examine it.'

But the Vizier spat in his face and cried: 'Miserable old fool, do you expect me to remain your servant when I can be your master?'

So saying, the Vizier rubbed the ring and said to the jinnee: 'Take up this wretch and cast him down by the side of his cobbler son-in-law!'

The jinnee at once carried the old man upon his shoulder and, flying with him through the void, set him down in the middle of the desert, where King and son-in-law sat wailing together. So much for them.

The Vizier summoned the nobles and the captains of the troops and proclaimed himself Sultan of the city. He explained that he had banished the King and Ma'aruf by the power of a magic ring, and threatened the assembly, saying: 'If anyone dares resist my rule, he shall join them in the desert of hunger and thirst!'

Perforce the courtiers swore fealty, and the Vizier, after exalting some and dismissing others, sent to the Princess, saying: 'Prepare to receive me this night, for my heart yearns for you!'

The Princess, who was stricken with grief at the downfall of her father and Ma'aruf, sent back to say: 'I cannot receive you until you have drawn up a marriage-contract and become my lawful husband.' But the Vizier replied: 'I know nothing of marriage-contracts, and accept no such excuses. I desire to visit you at once.'

'Come, then, you will be welcome,' answered the Princess through her eunuch.

When evening came she arrayed herself in silks and jewels, perfumed herself, and received the Vizier with a seductive smile. 'What an honour, my master,' she said. 'What a night we shall pass together!'

She seated him on her couch and dallied with him until he was roused to a frenzy of desire. But as he was about to throw himself upon her, she uttered a cry of terror and started back, covering her face.

'What is the matter, my mistress?' asked the Vizier.

'Would you show me naked to that stranger?' she cried.

'Where? Where?' exclaimed the Vizier angrily.

'There, in your ring!' she answered.

The Vizier laughed and said: 'Dear lady, that is no man, but only my faithful jinnee.'

But the Princess screamed still louder and cried: 'I am terrified of jinn! Put him away, for my sake!'

Impatient to do that for which he had come, the Vizier took off the ring from his finger and hid it under the cushions. The Princess let him approach and, when he had come near, kicked him so violently in the belly that he rolled over senseless on the floor. Thereupon she gave a loud cry, and at once forty slave-girls burst into the room and laid hold of the Vizier, whilst she hastily snatched up the ring and rubbed the seal, saying to the jinnee: 'Cast this traitor into a dark dungeon and bring me back my father and my husband!'

'I hear and obey!' replied the jinnee, and, carrying the Vizier on his shoulder, threw him in the darkest dungeon of the palace. Then he flew towards the desert and presently returned with the King and Ma'aruf, both half-dead with fright and hunger.

The Princess rejoiced to see them. She offered them food and wine and told them how she had outwitted the Vizier.

'We will tie him to the stake and burn him alive!' cried the King. 'But first give me back the ring, my daughter.'

But the Princess replied: 'The ring shall stay on my finger. I myself will look after it in future.'

Early next morning the King and Ma'aruf entered the council-chamber, and the courtiers, who were astonished to see them, kissed the ground before them and gave them a jubilant welcome. The stake was set up in the grounds of the palace and the Vizier was burnt alive in sight of all the people.

Ma'aruf was appointed Vizier and heir to the throne. He governed jointly with the King and lived happily with his wife, who after a few months gave birth to a son.

Five years later the King died, and soon the Princess followed him to eternal rest. Before she died she commended the young Prince to the care of Ma'aruf, and gave him the ring and counselled him to guard it well.

King Ma'aruf reigned wisely and justly for many years, so that all his subjects loved him. One night, however, when he had retired to his sleeping chamber, a hideous old woman jumped out of his bed and flung her arms around him.

'Allah preserve us from the wiles of the Evil One!' exclaimed Ma'aruf in terror. 'Who are you?'

'Have no fear!' replied the hag. 'I am your wife, Fatimah!'

Ma'aruf recognized her by her long teeth and her black ugliness. 'But how came you here?' he asked in amazement. 'Who brought you to this city?'

'Last night,' answered Fatimah, 'as I sat in a street by the wall of a ruined house, begging alms from the passers-by and bewailing my woeful plight, a jinnee appeared, saying: "Why are you weeping, old woman?" When I recounted to him my misfortunes since you left me and told him that my name was Fatimah, wife of Ma'aruf, one time cobbler in Red Lane, the jinnee said: "I know your husband. He is now King of Ikhtiyan-al-Khatan, and if you wish I will take you to him." The jinnee carried me upon his back and flew with me between earth and sky until he alighted on the roof of this palace and set me down upon your bed.'

The old shrew wept and, kneeling down before her husband, begged forgiveness of him. Ma'aruf took pity on his wife. He bade her rise and, seating her by his side, related to her all that had befallen him since his flight from Cairo. He set apart a magnificent palace for her use and assigned twenty slave-girls to her service.

When Fatimah saw, however, that her husband held aloof from her bed and sought his pleasure with other women, she became jealous and her evil soul prompted her to seek his ruin. One night, whilst Ma'aruf was fast asleep with the magic ring under his pillow, she entered the palace and stealthily made her way to his room. She softly approached her husband's bed and took the ring from under the pillow.

Now it so chanced that as she was stealing out, with the ring in her hand, Ma'aruf's son, the young Prince, was passing by the door of his father's room. He followed her unnoticed until she came to the vestibule of the palace. Here she slipped the ring on her finger and was about to rub the seal, when he drew his sword and struck her through the neck. With a piercing scream she dropped dead to the ground.

The young Prince hurried to his father's chamber and roused him from his sleep. Ma'aruf praised his son for his bravery and recovered the ring from his wife's finger. Then he called out to his attendants and ordered them to take the body and bury it in the grounds of the palace. Such was the end of Fatimah.

King Ma'aruf reigned through many joyful years, until he was visited by the Destroyer of all earthly pleasures, the Leveller of mighty kings and humble peasants.